I0782083

My Journey Into the Gospel

A Changed Man

by

Devin M. Nelson, Sr.

My Journey Into the Gospel

Copyright © 2025 Devin M. Nelson, Sr.

Printed by USA Book Promoters in the United States of America.

First printing edition 2025.

Dedication

My Journey Into the Gospel: A Changed Man is dedicated to my mother, Lucy Nelson (Rest in Paradise - December 2012), and my stepmother, April Darget (Rest in Paradise - October 2017).

To my father, Leon Darget, and my cousin, Antonio Allen Jr., thank you for believing in me and supporting this project.

To my five children, Alissa Dawkins, Anastasia Scott, Devin Jr., Destiny and Da'mir Nelson—thank you for being my inspiration. And to their mothers, Andrea Dawkins, LaQuisha Scott, and Charveta Jackson—I am a changed man because of all of you.

Acknowledgment

I extend my heartfelt thanks to Karen E. Williams and Tina Rowell, who welcomed me when I felt lost and abandoned.

To my Pastor, Mike Osminski, thank you for guiding me at the start of my rededication journey, and to the Lord of the Harvest Fellowship, our church family. I am also grateful to Chaplain Bossardet who continues to be part of our blessings, and to the Kingdom Community and the Sons of God choir.

I would also like to express my gratitude to Ajetta Morgan, Sharonda Lee, Marsharee Reed, Antonio Allen, Jr., Judy Lever (Nelson), Alonzo White, and all who continue to believe in me—you are not alone. I will return physically; I am with you in spirit, emotion, and mind.

Special thanks to the team at *USA Book Promoters* for supporting and publishing my manuscript.

Contents

Introduction

Yahshua Prayer

Our Father in Heaven,

hallowed be Your name,

Your kingdom come,

Your will be done,

on earth as in heaven.

Give us today our daily bread.

Forgive us our sins as we forgive those who sin against us. Save us from the time of trial, and deliver us from evil.

For the kingdom, the power, and the glory are Yours,

now and forever. Amen!

Serenity Prayer

"Father! Grant me the serenity to accept the things I cannot change, the courage to change the things I can, and the wisdom to know the difference."

Living one day at a time, enjoying one moment at a time, accepting hardships as the pathway to peace. Taking, as our Savior did, this sinful world as it is, not as I would have it.

Trusting that all things are to be right if I surrender to His will.

That I may be reasonably happy in this life and supremely happy in the next, forever! Amen!

<u>Shepherd's Prayer</u>

"Yahweh is my Shepherd; I shall not want.

He makes me lie down in green pastures;

He leads me beside still waters.

He restores my soul;

He leads me in the path of righteousness for His name's sake.

Though I walk through the valley of the shadow of death,

I will fear no evil, for You are with me;

Your rod and Your staff they comfort me.

You prepare a table for me in the presence of my enemies;

You anoint my head with oil, my cup runs over.

Goodness and mercy shall follow me all the days of my life;

And I will dwell in the house of Yahweh forever and ever. Amen!"

Sometimes, we aren't raised in the best conditions or environments. Many of us have faced poverty or even worse hardships.

It is out of free will that we accept Yahshua as our Savior, that we accept Yahweh as our Heavenly Father. We were created in His image to receive love and experience an abundant life through obedience and love of Him. Our past does not define our future; in the present, we must seek true and meaningful change.

Yahweh left instructions intended to bring love, greatness, and prosperity. These promises reveal how we should live, the path to salvation, the fate of sinners, and the joy of those who believe in Yahshua. Throughout history, Yahweh's instructions have been called many things—Holy Doctrine, Binding Precepts, True History, and Immutable Decisions. Yahweh's instructions are believed to be wise, live safe, and practiced to receive the Holy Spirit, direct light, support the Word, and bring comfort, promise, and cheer to life.

These instructions for life were described as the traveler's map, the pilgrim's staff, the pilot's compass, the soldier's sword, and the very essence of the Holy Spirit. They are believed to restore paradise, open the gates of Heaven, close the gates of Hell, serve good, overcome evil, and cultivate a positive spirit.

They should be read slowly to be understood, frequently to be protected, and prayerfully for a wealthy mind. These ways lead to paradise in glory, rivers of flowing pleasure, high responsibility, and the rewards of the laborer. So, taking from or adding to these instructions will be condemned by the Holy Trinity.

These ways were established to provide aid in times of need, guidance through life's challenges, protection for survival in the world, strength to overcome obstacles, and a path for repentance and prayer when we fall short.

1

Scripture

A friend will always love you, and a brother is born for a time of adversity.[1] Love Yahweh with all your heart, soul, mind, and strength. Love your neighbor as yourself,[2] and you will receive Yahweh's promise.

A half-dead man was once in need of a brother to help him. That brother came to his aid, bandaged his wounds, sought additional help, and ensured he was well before moving on.[3]

Joy must remain in our hearts, and we must love one another as Yahweh loves us. Yahshua called us friends so that we might know the promises of Yahweh and anything we ask of Yahshua, Yahweh will provide. Our obedience is meant to produce good fruit, blessings, and the offspring of love as we receive our sisters and brothers through Yahweh and assist them.

In aiding our brothers, we become helpers, for they were created so that men would not be alone in life. Our Rod is the Father, the Stem is the mother, and the Branch is the children who grow out of the roots of their parents.

Yahweh will not judge by what He sees or hears but by righteousness. The rod of His mouth will strike the earth, and His breath will slay the wicked. Righteousness is His belt, and faithfulness is the belt around His waist.[4]

They will not harm Yahshua's mountain. The earth will be filled with the knowledge of Yahweh as the waters cover the sea,[5] and His

---

[1] Proverbs 17:17
[2] Mark 12:30-31
[3] Luke 10:30-37
[4] Isaiah 11:3-5
[5] Isaiah 11:9-11

truth will spread across the land.[6] A king will reign in righteousness, and a prince will rule with justice. A man will be a shelter from the wind, a refuge from the storm, like rivers of water in a dry place, and the shadow of a great rock in a weary land[7].

The eyes of those who see will no longer be dim, and those with ears will listen. The rash-hearted will gain understanding, and those with stammering tongues will speak plainly. Fools will no longer be considered noble; they will speak foolishness. Works will be preached in iniquity and ungodliness, error against Yahweh, and keeping the hungry unsatisfied and the thirsty will have no drink.[8]

Schemers are evil. They have wicked plans. Lying words will destroy the poor as the needy tries to speak justice. A generous man will do generous things as he stands on generosity.[9] If a faithful man desires the office of bishop, he desires a noble task. Now, a bishop should be above reproach, the husband of one wife, temperate, sober-minded, showing good behavior, hospitable, able to teach, not weak to wine, violence, or greed. He must be gentle, not quarrelsome or covetous. He has rules for his children to follow and is able to rule his house and the church. He must not be a recent convert, or he may be conceited and fall into the condemnation of the devil.[10] He must have a good testimony among those outside the church so as not to fall into reproach and the snare of the devil.

Do not use words to gain profit from or manipulate those who listen. Do your best to present yourself to God as one approved, a workman who has no need to be ashamed, rightly handling the word of truth.[11] Put to death the earthly practices of fornication, uncleanness,

---

[6] Matthew 24:14

[7] Isaiah 32:1-2

[8] Isaiah 32:3-6

[9] Isaiah 32:7-8

[10] 1 Timothy 3:1-7

[11] 2 Timothy 2:14-15

passion, evil desire, and idolatry, for the wrath of Yahweh is coming upon the disobedient.[12]

Put off the old self with its anger, malice, wrath, blasphemy, and harsh language. Do not lie to one another. Instead, put on the new self, renewed in knowledge according to the image of Yahweh. In Yahshua, there is no separation of any kind, for He is all and in all.[13]

As Yahweh's chosen ones, holy and beloved, put on compassion, kindness, humility, meekness, and patience, bear with one another and forgive one another, as the Lord has forgiven you. If anyone has a complaint against another, forgive them as Yahweh forgives us. Above all, put on love, which binds us together in perfect unity, and let the peace of Yahweh rule in your hearts, for we are called to be one body. And be thankful.[14]

Let the word of Yahweh dwell richly within you, with all wisdom, teaching, and admonishing one another in psalms, hymns, and spiritual songs, singing with thankfulness in your hearts to Yahweh. And whatever we do, in word or deed, we must do it all in the name of Yahshua, giving thanks to Yahweh through Him.[15]

---

[12] Colossians 3:5-6

[13] Ephesians 4:22-24

[14] Colossians 3:12-14

[15] Colossians 3:15-17

2
Learned Prayers

Trusting Yahweh

You are wonderful; there is nothing You can't fix, nothing You can't do. No problem is too great for You to solve; no need is beyond Your reach; there is no issue too great for You. I'm casting all my care upon You; I'm giving it all to You; I'm giving all of me to You. I'm laying my head upon Your chest…

Father! I know You love me… and I'm relying on You to provide for me all that I need! I am not going to be depressed, I am not going to stress out, I am not going to have a nervous breakdown. I am going to trust in You to defeat my enemies for Your glory. I am trusting You to break down the doors that are locked for the great of my behalf. I am relying on You to win the victory! Father, the problem is within me! Fix me, Father! Show me what I must do to be forgiven and healed by You and to be free to forgive others. Heal my relationships with everyone who supports, loves, and cares for me, those who look up to me as I look up to You, Father. I depend entirely on You, Father!

Single Man

Most gracious and loving Heavenly Father, I come into Your presence with gratitude, knowing that I am somebody in Your eyes. I thank You for the happiness and prosperity I experience as a single man because of Your favor and blessings on my life. Father, I ask You to saturate my life completely with Your presence, to guide me, and to help me find my purpose in You. I feel a deep sense of destiny and a future waiting to manifest in my life, and I am secure and confident in the One who lives within me, giving me the supernatural strength to abstain from any premarital sexual relationship. I know that such actions would destroy the intimacy and fellowship I have with You and hinder my future relationship with my wife.

Help me, Father, to always remain open-minded in all relationships and to seek Your will and do what is right in them, particularly in a marriage relationship. If the day comes for me to marry, I pray that You will bring me the wife You have chosen for me, just as You created Eve for Adam. Until that day, Father, I thank You that whenever I feel lonely, I can talk to You in prayer and find comfort in Your word. Thank You, Father, for being my friend and accepting all of me.

<u>Falling Short</u>

Father! I come to You with a heart full of gratitude for Your loving-kindness. I thank You that even though I have made wrong decisions in my life that led me away from You and faithfulness, Your faithfulness remains steadfast within me, and You still love me. Though my fellowship with You was broken, Christ is still my Savior. I am truly sorry for all my sins and weary of living in remorse for what has been done. I repent of my sins and humbly ask for Your forgiveness.

I am grateful that Your forgiveness and mercy do not depend on my good works but are made available to me through Your grace. I rejoice that Your mercy endures forever and is renewed every morning! Thank Yahshua for forgiving me and receiving me back into fellowship with You. Today, I make a wholehearted commitment to You and Your Word. Thank You for giving me Your Spirit, who grants me the divine strength and grace to avoid the things in my life that previously caused me to stumble and fall. Help me to take it one day at a time, trusting in Your grace and mercy to guide me through every moment, temptation, and trial.

Thank You for restoring the fullness of Your joy to my heart and soul as I walk in fellowship with You. I know that whenever I feel insecure and unfulfilled, I will find strength in Your courage and wisdom. Thank You for the restoration of our fellowship and for renewing the joy in my heart as Your child.

Business Man

Father! I ask for Your wisdom in all my decisions, knowledge in all my transactions, and understanding in all my dealings related to my business. Keep me from being deceived into illegal transactions and help me to set my heart on walking in integrity, regardless of any monetary gain. I understand that true prosperity comes from maintaining purity in my motives and conducting my business with honesty. I commit myself to this, Father.

Father! Help me resist the temptation to climb the ladder of success by stepping on others. I pray that I do not become so consumed by my work that I forget my primary purpose in You is to minister to those around me. I thank You for the supernatural strength You provide, which overcomes all stress and anxiety.

Finally, I thank You for blessing any business that seeks prosperity through Your guidance. As I place You first in every area of my life, including my profession, we are in a covenant together. I expect the windows of opportunity to open for my business and for Your great blessings to manifest in my life.

May these blessings then spread to others through the preaching and teaching of the Gospel. I now see the truth and greatness of Your help, Father.

Salvation

Father, have mercy on me, a sinner. I confess my sins, acknowledging them with a heavy heart. I am not proud of my transgressions, but I recognize them and seek Your forgiveness. I thank You for dying to reclaim those who have fallen and need redemption. I am one such person. I humbly ask You to forgive me, cleanse me of my unrighteousness, and transform me into the man You have destined me to be—the man with a purpose in Your plan.

I accept Yahshua as my Savior and ask Him to save every area of struggle in my life. I rejoice that His blood cleanses me from all sin.

Even as I pray, I am filled with the Holy Spirit. I dedicate my life to You and commit to living each day according to Your Word. Thank You for granting me a second chance as Your Spirit and Word reign in my life. I rise to serve You for the rest of my days.

A Prisoner

Father, I come to You in prayer with a grateful heart. Despite the many mistakes I have made, You are the Savior of forgiveness. I seek Your forgiveness and commit to dedicating my life to You, to following Your will, and to fulfilling Your purpose for me.

I trust that You have forgiven all my wrongdoings, even though I sometimes struggle to forgive myself. Help me to understand that I cannot change the past, but I can shape my present and hope for a better future. I surrender all bitterness, loneliness, and low self-esteem to You. I forgive those who have hurt me and extend forgiveness to myself for the mistakes and sins of my past.

By Your grace, I will use this time of imprisonment to study, pray, and deepen my personal commitment to You. Rather than viewing this period as a crushing defeat, I will see it as a stepping stone to greater achievement.

Prepare me to re-enter society with a sense of responsibility, having learned from my experiences and mistakes. Most of all, thank You, Father, for loving me and looking beyond my faults.

Purity

Father, I acknowledge my own wretchedness and recognize the areas of my life that need correction. I refuse to place the blame on others. With a sincere heart, I repent and turn away from these sins as a commitment of my will. Grant me the grace to overcome every lustful addiction that enslaves me. I need Your touch to cleanse me. Wash my thoughts, deeds, and even my memories so that I may serve You with purity and holiness. I am grateful for Yahshua's sacrifice, which delivers me from every bondage and fulfills my desire to be free. Thank You for Your Word, which cleanses me from all unrighteousness. I commit to renewing my mind and hiding Your Word in my heart so that I may serve You without guilt, in the freedom and power of Your Holy Spirit.

Refuge

Father! You are beneficent and merciful!

I seek refuge from anxiety and depression,

I seek refuge from laziness and lack of strength, I seek refuge from cowardice and ignorance,

I seek refuge from debt and the oppression of man.

Father! Suffice me with what is lawful to keep me away from what is prohibited and, with grace, make me free of want of what is beside me.

My Marriage

Father! Blessed be Your name forever! May the heavens and all Your creation praise You eternally. You created Adam and gave him Eve as his wife and helper. Bless me with Your beautiful creation 'woman' as my wife, not with lust but with love as we are one another's helper; join us together as one and send down Your mercy on us, grant that we may grow old together as we become one.

You said, "It is not good for man to be alone, let's make him a helper,"[16] and what you have "joined together, no one should ever separate."[17]

Blessed are Your holy angels who watch over us. Unite us and bless these angels as they guide and protect us throughout all ages. Though I have been afflicted, I have also experienced Your mercy.

---

[16] Genesis 2:18

[17] Matthew 19:6

Now, I seek Your grace for my future wife and me. Once, I was lost, but now I see clearly Your blessings. Father, please bless our marriage.

While I am incarcerated, my hope is to be reunited with my children and live rightly by honoring all who are part of my life through the guidance of the Holy Trinity.

HE

ONLY

LEFT

YOU

BASIC

INSTRUCTIONS

BEFORE

LEAVING

EARTH

3

Yahweh and Believers

"If you love me, you will keep my commandments."

(John 14:15)

"You have made known to me the path of life; You fill me with joy in Your presence with eternal pleasure at Your right hand."

(Psalm 16:11)

"I pray that out of His glorious riches, He may strengthen you with power through His Spirit in your inner being."

(Ephesians 3:16)

"My soul is consumed with longing for Your laws at all times."

(Psalm 119:20)

"Do nothing out of selfish ambition or vain conceit, but in humility consider others better than yourselves."

(Philippians 2:3)

"Each of you should look not only to your own interest, but also to the interest of others."

(Philippians 2:4)

"If you keep biting and devouring each other, watch out, or you will be destroyed by each other."

(Galatians 5:15)

"Confess your sins to each other and pray for one another so you may be healed."

(James 5:16)

"He has made us complete as ministers of a new covenant not of the law but the spirit; for the law kills but the spirit gives life."

(2 Corinthians 3:6)

"The fruit of the Spirit is love, joy, peace, patience, kindness, goodness, faithfulness, gentleness, and self-control."

(Galatians 5:22-23)

"Do not keep talking so proudly or let your mouth speak such arrogance, for the Father knows, by Him deeds are weighed."

(1 Samuel 2:3)

"Yahweh oppresses the proud but gives grace to the humble. Therefore, humble yourselves under Yahweh's mighty hand that He may lift you up."

(1 Peter 5:5-6)

"May Yahweh, the source of hope, fill you with joy and peace as you believe in Him so that you may overflow with hope by the power of the Holy Spirit."

(Romans 15:13)

"Set your minds on things above, not material things, for you have died and your life is hidden with Christ in Yahweh."

(Colossians 3:2-3)

"Anyone who is a friend of the world is not a friend of Yahweh."

(James 4:4)

"Though you have not seen Him, you love Him, and even though you do not see Him, you believe in Him and are filled with glory and joy."

(Peter 1:8)

"What is seen is temporary, and what is unseen is eternal."

Corinthians 4:18)

"I will praise Yahweh all my life; I will sing praise to my Creator as long as I live."

(Psalm 104:33)

"I set Yahweh always before me; I will not be shaken."

(Psalm 16:8)

"If you think you are standing firm, be careful not to fall."

(1 Corinthians 10:12)

"Trust in Yahweh with all your heart and lean not on your own understanding; acknowledge Him, and He will make paths straight."

(Proverbs 3:5-6)

"I have been crucified with Yahshua; I no longer live; Yahshua lives in me."

(Galatians 2:20)

"Whatever you have learned, received, or heard from me or seen in me—put it into practice; Yahshua of peace will be with you."

(Philippians 4:9)

"Yahshua may dwell in your hearts through faith; I pray you be rooted and established in love, having power together with all saints to grasp how wide, long, high, and deep the love of Yahshua is, this love surpasses, knowledge is Yahweh."

(Ephesians 3:17-19)

"My flesh and my heart may fail; Yahweh is my strength of heart and my portion forever."

(Psalm 73:26)

My soul thirsts for Yahweh and Yahshua; the heavens declare the glory of Yahweh, the skies proclaim the works of His hands."

(Psalm 19:1)

"I will praise You, Father, with all my heart I will tell of Your wonders."

(Psalm 9:1)

"Yours, Yahweh, is the greatness, the power, the glory, the majesty, and the splendor for everything in Heaven and earth is Yours."

(1 Chronicles 29:11)

"Glory in his holy name; let the hearts of those who seek the LORD rejoice!"

(1 Chronicles 16:10)

"Be joyful always, pray continually, give thanks in all circumstances, for this is Yahweh's will for you."

(1 Thessalonians 5:16-18)

"Do not be anxious about anything, but in everything by prayer and petition with thanksgiving present your request to Yahweh."

(Philippians 4:6)

"The peace of Yahshua which transcends all understanding will guard your hearts and your minds in Yahshua."

(Philippians 4:7)

"The LORD your God is with you. He is mighty to save you, he will take great delight in you, he will quiet you with his love, he will rejoice over you with singing."

(Zephaniah 3:17)

"Blessed are those who have learned to acclaim You, who walk in the light of Your presence, Yahweh, they rejoice in Your name all day long; they exult in Your righteousness."

(Psalm 89:15-16)

"Create in me a pure heart, Father, and renew steadfast love and a clean spirit within me. Do not cast me from your presence or take your Holy Spirit from me; restore to me the joy of your salvation and grant me a willing spirit."

(Psalm 51:10-12)

"May all who seek You rejoice and be glad in You, may those who love Your salvation always say, Father be exalted."

(Psalm 40:16)

"My soul will delight in His salvation and rejoice in Yahshua."

(Psalm 35:9)

"You turned my wailing into dancing; You removed my sackcloth and clothed me with joy."

(Psalm 30:11)

"Yahshua is my light and salvation, whom shall I fear, Yahshua is the stronghold of my life, whom shall I be afraid."

(Psalm 27:1)

"You have made known to me the path of life; You will fill me with joy in Your presence with eternal pleasure at Your right hand."

(Psalm 16:11)

"Glory in His holy name; let the hearts of those who seek the LORD rejoice."

(Psalm 105:3)

4

Yahweh and Yahshua

Demonstrating His immense love for us, Yahshua died for us while we were still sinners.[18] As the Messiah, He promised rest to all who come to Him, weary from their labors.[19] Though all have sinned and fall short of His glory,[20] His sacrifice brought joy to many. While the wages of sin is death, the gift of eternal life comes from Yahweh through Yahshua.[21] Whoever believes in the Word, hears it, and trusts in Yahweh, who sent Yahshua, has everlasting life and will not face judgment from Yahweh.[22]

Whoever causes one of these little ones who believe in Me to sin, it would be better for him if a great millstone were hung around his neck and he were thrown into the sea.[23] Because of sexual immorality, each man should have one wife and each woman one husband, and they should fulfill their conjugal duties to one another.

Yahweh gives us a spirit of power, love, and self-control, not fear.[24] Yahshua delivers us from all fears; when we are afraid, we can place our trust in Yahweh through Him.[25] Everyone who practices sin is a slave to sin and does not remain in the house forever; Yahshua remains forever. Therefore, if we are set free, it is by Him.[26]

---

[18] Romans 5:8

[19] Matthew 11:28

[20] Romans 3:23

[21] Romans 6:23

[22] John 3:16

[23] Matthew 18:6

[24] 2 Timothy 1:7

[25] Psalm 34:4

[26] John 8:34-36

Yahshua is not tempted by evil; rather, temptation arises from our own evil desires, luring and enticing us.[27] When these desires mature, they bring forth death.

Do not be anxious about what you will eat, drink, or wear. Instead, seek first the kingdom of Yahweh, and all these things will be added to you. Do not be anxious about anything, but in everything, by prayer and supplication with thanksgiving, let your requests be made known to Yahshua.[28] Our hearts and minds are guarded by Yahshua, and Yahweh is our refuge and strength, a very present help in trouble.[29]

The darkness will pass away, and true light will shine. Whoever is in the light must help his brethren who are still in darkness. Have mercy, Yahweh, according to Your unfailing love.[30]

Husbands must love their wives and not be harsh with them, striving for peace and holiness to see Yahweh. Ensure that no one fails to obtain the grace of Yahweh and that no root of bitterness springs up to cause trouble or defilement.[31]

If you forgive others their trespasses, Yahweh will also forgive you. If you do not forgive others, Yahweh will not forgive you.[32] Do not judge or despise your brothers; we all stand before the judgment seat of Yahweh. Therefore, do not pass judgment on one another any longer, and decide never to place a stumbling block or hindrance in a brother's way. We all fall short.[33]

---

[27] James 1:13-14

[28] Matthew 6:31-33

[29] Philippians 4:7

[30] Psalm 51:1

[31] Ephesians 5:25-27

[32] Matthew 6:14-15

[33] Matthew 7:1-5

In the beginning was the Word, and the Word was with Yahweh, and the Word was Yahweh. All things were made through Him, and in Him was life and the light of men.[34]

Yahshua said, "I am the way, the truth, and the life; no one comes to Yahweh except through Me."[35]

If anyone lacks wisdom, let him ask Yahweh, who gives generously to all without reproach, and it will be given to him.[36] Neither death, life, angels, rulers, things present, things to come, powers, height, depth, nor anything else in all creation will be able to separate us from the love of Yahweh.[37]

Yahshua said, "I am the resurrection and the life; if you believe in Me, though you die, you will live."[38] Where, O death, is your victory? Where, O death, is your sting? The sting of death is sin, and the power of sin is the law. Yahweh gives us victory through Yahshua. Therefore, brothers, be steadfast, immovable, and always abounding in the work of Yahweh, knowing that your labor is not in vain.[39]

We do not want you to be uninformed about those who are asleep so that you do not grieve like those who have no hope. We believe that Yahshua died and rose again; therefore, through Yahshua, Yahweh will bring with Him those who have fallen asleep.[40]

For we declare to you by the word of Yahweh that we who are alive, who remain until the coming of Yahweh, will not precede those who have fallen asleep. Yahweh will descend from heaven with a cry of command, with the voice of an archangel, and with the sound of a trumpet. The dead in Yahshua will rise first. Then we who are alive and remain will be caught up together with them in the clouds to meet

---

[34] John 1:1-4

[35] John 14:6

[36] James 1:5

[37] Romans 8:38-39

[38] John 11:25

[39] 1 Corinthians 15:55-58

[40] 1 Thessalonians 4:13-14

Yahweh in the air. And so, we will always be with Yahweh. Therefore, encourage one another with these words.[41]

He answered and delivered me from all my fears. I waited patiently for Him; He inclined to me and heard my cry. He drew me up from the pit of destruction, out of the miry clay, and set my feet upon a rock, making my steps secure. I will hope in Him and praise Him again as my salvation and Father.[42]

I call to Yahshua, and Yahweh saves me. Evening and morning, and at noon, I utter my complaint and moan, and He hears my voice.[43] Cast your burdens on Him, and He will sustain you; He will never permit the righteous to be moved.[44] He who dwells in the shelter of the Most High will abide in the shadow of the Almighty. I will say of Him, "The Father is on my side; I will not fear. What can man do to me?"[45]

We are afflicted in every way but not crushed, perplexed but not driven to despair.[46] We do not lose heart; though our outer self is wasting away, our inner self is being renewed day by day.[47] He is the image of the invisible Father, the firstborn of all creation. By Him, all things were created in heaven and on earth, visible and invisible— whether thrones or dominions, rulers or authorities—all things were created through Him and for Him. He is before all things, and in Him, all things hold together.[48]

What, then, shall we say to these things? If Yahshua is for us, who can be against us?[49] Who shall separate us from the love of Yahshua?

____

[41] 1 Thessalonians 4:15-18

[42] Psalm 40:1-3

[43] Psalm 55:16-17

[44] Psalm 55:22

[45] Psalm 91:1-2

[46] 2 Corinthians 4:8

[47] 2 Corinthians 4:16

[48] Colossians 1:15-17

[49] Romans 8:31

Shall tribulation, distress, persecution, famine, nakedness, danger, or sword?[50]

Yahweh loved us so much that He gave us His only Son, that whoever believes in Him should not perish but have eternal life.[51] If your brother sins, rebuke him, and if he repents, forgive him.[52] If he sins against you seven times and turns to you seven times, forgive him every time.[53]

At my first defense, no one came to stand by me; all deserted me. May it not be charged against them. But Yahweh stood by me and strengthened me, so that through me the message might be fully proclaimed, and all the Gentiles might hear it. Yahweh will rescue me from every evil deed and bring me safely into His heavenly kingdom. To Him be the glory forever and ever.[54]

A man of many companions may come to ruin, but there is a friend who sticks closer than a brother—Yahshua![55] Do not be anxious about tomorrow; tomorrow will be anxious for itself. Today has enough trouble of its own.[56] You do not know what tomorrow will bring;[57] whatever Yahshua wills, that will be.[58] We are temporary.

Solomon, in all his glory, was not arrayed like one of the flowers of the field, which today is alive and tomorrow is thrown into the oven. Will He not much more clothe you?[59] The love of money is the root of all evil. It is through this craving that some have wandered away from the faith and pierced themselves with many sorrows.[60] Keep your

---

[50] Romans 8:38

[51] John 3:16

[52] Matthew 18:15

[53] Matthew 18:21-22

[54] 2 Timothy 4:16-18

[55] Proverbs 19:24

[56] Matthew 6:34

[57] Proverbs 27:1

[58] James 4:15

[59] Matthew 6:29-30

[60] 1 Timothy 6:11

life free from the love of money and be content with what you have, for He will never leave you or forsake you.[61]

I will instruct you and teach you in the way you should go;

I will counsel you with My eye upon you.[62] Commit your way to Yahweh; trust in Him, and He will act. [63] Whoever conceals his transgressions will not prosper, but he who confesses and forsakes his sins will obtain mercy.[64]

Yahweh, You have searched me and known me. You discern my thoughts from afar; You search out my path, and my lying down and are acquainted with all my ways.[65] Keep my words and treasure my commandments. Keep my commands and live; keep my teaching as the apple of your eye; bind them on your fingers; write them on your heart.[66]

When my father and mother forsake me, Yahweh will take me in.[67] In Him I trust; make known the way I should follow,[68] for to You I lift my soul, casting all my anxieties on Him forever.[69]

"In My Father's house are many rooms; if it were not so, I would have told you. I go to prepare a place for you. If I go and prepare a place for you, I will come again and take you to Myself, that where I am, you may be also. You know the way to where I am going."[70] "Peace, I leave with you; My peace I give to you, not as the world gives. Do not let your heart be troubled, neither let it be afraid."[71]

---

[61] Hebrews 13:5

[62] Psalm 32:8

[63] Proverbs 16:3

[64] Proverbs 28:13

[65] Psalm 139:1-3

[66] Proverbs 7:1-3

[67] Psalm 27:10

[68] Proverbs 22:19

[69] Psalm 25:1-3

[70] John 14:2-4

[71] John 14:27-28

In the world, you will have many tribulations, but take heart. Yahshua has overcome the world. Therefore, since we have been justified by faith, we have peace with Yahweh through Yahshua.[72] Through Him, we have obtained access by faith to this grace in which we stand, and we rejoice in the hope of the glory of Yahweh. Rejoice even in suffering, knowing that suffering produces endurance, endurance produces character, and character produces hope. Hope does not put us to shame because His love has been poured into our hearts through the Holy Spirit, who has been given to us for guidance.[73]

Do not be deceived: "Bad company ruins good morals." [74] Whoever walks with the wise becomes wise, but the companion of fools suffers harm.[75] A friend loves at all times, and a brother is born for adversity.[76]

Everyone who looks at a woman with lustful intent has already committed adultery in his heart. [77] For this reason, dishonorable passions were created in the contrary exchange of nature. Shameless acts arose when men received other men as women—this is an error and a penalty. [78] Our bodies are temples and gifts from Yahweh, containing the Holy Spirit.[79] Therefore, flee from passion and pursue righteousness, faith, love, and peace, along with those who call on Yahweh from a pure heart and mind.[80]

"My grace is sufficient for you, for My power is made perfect in weakness." Therefore, I will boast gladly of my weaknesses so that the power of Messiah may rest upon me. For the sake of Messiah, I am content with weaknesses, insults, hardships, persecutions, and

---

[72] John 16:33

[73] Romans 5:1-5

[74] 1 Corinthians 15:33

[75] Proverbs 13:20

[76] Proverbs 17:17

[77] Matthew 5:28

[78] Romans 2:26-27

[79] 1 Corinthians 6:19

[80] 2 Timothy 2:22

calamities. For when I am weak, then I am strong.[81] If any among us is sick, let him call for the elders of the church to pray over him and anoint his head with oil in the name of Yahshua. The prayer of faith will save the sick person, and Yahweh will raise him up. If he has committed sins, he will be forgiven by Yahweh.[82]

Blessed be Yahweh and Yahshua, the source of mercies and all comfort, who comforts us in all our afflictions so that we may be able to comfort those who are in any affliction with the same comfort we have received.[83]

Yahweh is near the brokenhearted and saves the crushed in spirit.[84] He will hide me in His shelter in the day of trouble; He will conceal me under the cover of His tent and lift me high upon a rock.[85] For His anger is but for a moment, but His favor is for a lifetime. Weeping may last through the night, but joy comes with the morning.[86] Be still before Yahweh and wait patiently for Him; do not fret over those who prosper in their way or the man who carries out evil devices. Refrain from anger, forsake wrath, and do not give in to evil.[87]

Answer me quickly, Yahweh! My spirit fails; do not hide Your face from me, lest I become like those who go down to the pit.[88] Deliver me from my enemies; I have fled to You for refuge. Teach me to do Your will, for You are Yahweh. Let the Holy Spirit lead me on level ground and preserve my life. Bring my soul out of trouble.[89] Let anyone who thinks he stands take heed lest he fall. No temptation has overtaken you that is not common to man. Yahshua is faithful; He will not let you be tempted beyond your ability but will provide a way of

---

[81] 2 Corinthians 12:9-10
[82] James 5:14-15
[83] 2 Corinthians 1:3-4
[84] Psalm 35:18
[85] 3 Psalm 27:5
[86] Psalm 30:4-5
[87] Psalm 37:7-8
[88] Psalm 143:7
[89] Psalm 143:9-11

escape.[90] Flee from evil, submit to Yahweh, and resist Satan, and he will flee from you.[91]

May Yahweh answer you in the day of trouble! May Yahweh protect you! May He send you help from the sanctuary and grant you support from Zion![92] In You, Father, I take refuge; let me not be put to shame! In Your righteousness, deliver and rescue me; listen to me![93]

Take My yoke upon you and learn from Me, for I am gentle and lowly in heart, and you will find rest for your soul. My yoke is easy, and My burden is light.[94] Let us not grow weary of doing good, for in due season, we will reap a harvest if we do not give up.[95]

You knit me together in my mother's womb. I praise You because I am wonderfully made; Your works are marvelous, and my soul knows it very well. My frame was not hidden from You; I was being made in secret, intricately woven together in the depths of the earth. Your eyes saw my unformed substance. In Your book were written the days that were formed for me when as yet there were none.[96]

---

[90] 1 Corinthians 10:12-13

[91] James 4:7

[92] Psalm 20:1-2

[93] Psalm 31:1-2

[94] Matthew 11:29-30

[95] Galatians 6:9

[96] Psalm 139:13-16

5

Knowledge of The Gospel

Do not lay up for yourselves treasures on earth, where moth and rust destroy and where thieves break in and steal. Instead, lay up for yourselves treasures in heaven, where neither moth nor rust destroys and where thieves do not break in and steal. For where your treasure is, there your heart will be also. The eye is the lamp of the body. If your eye is healthy, your whole body will be full of light. But if your eye is unhealthy, your whole body will be full of darkness.[97]

No one can serve two masters. He will either hate the one and love the other or be devoted to one and despise the other. You cannot serve both Yahweh and Satan.[98] Life is more than food, and the body is more than clothing. Consider the lilies of the field: they grow and neither toil nor spin, yet I tell you that even Solomon, in all his glory, was not arrayed like one of these. If Yahweh so clothes the grass of the field, which is alive today and tomorrow, is thrown into the oven, will He not much more clothe you?[99]

Gentiles seek after all these things, yet Yahweh knows all that you need. Therefore, humble yourselves under the mighty hand of Yahweh so that at the proper time, He may exalt you.[100] Rejoice, though now, for a little while, if necessary, you have been grieved by various trials. These trials serve to test your genuine faith, which is more precious than gold that perishes, even though it is tested by fire. Your faith may be found to result in praise, glory, and honor at the revelation of Yahshua.[101]

---

[97] Matthew 6:19-22

[98] Matthew 6:24

[99] Matthew 6:25b-9

[100] Matthew 6:23—33

[101] 1 Peter 6-8

Repay no evil for evil, but give thought to doing what is honorable in the sight of all. If possible, so far as it depends on you, live peacefully.[102] Do not be overcome by evil, but overcome evil with good.[103] Be angry, but do not sin; do not let the sun go down on your anger.[104] A soft answer turns away wrath, but a harsh word stirs up anger.[105] Good sense makes one slow to anger, and it is glorious to overlook an offense.[106]

Whoever divorces his or her spouse should provide a certificate of divorce. However, anyone who divorces his or her spouse, except for reasons of sexual immorality, causes them to commit adultery, and whoever marries someone who has been divorced commits adultery.[107]

The soul of the sluggard craves and gets nothing, but the soul of the diligent is richly supplied.[108] Yahweh will wipe away every tear from their eyes; death will be no more, neither mourning, nor crying, nor pain, for the former things have passed away.[109]

I will remember their sins and their lawless deeds no more.[110] I acknowledge my sins to You and did not cover my iniquity. I will confess my transgressions to Yahweh, and You forgave the guilt of my sin.[111] Let us hold fast to the confession of our hope without wavering, for He who promised is faithful.[112] "My sheep hear my voice, and I know them, and they follow me. I give them eternal life, and they will never perish. No one will snatch them out of my hand."[113]

---

[102] Romans 12:17-18

[103] Romans 12:21

[104] Ephesians 4:26

[105] Proverbs 15:1

[106] Proverbs 19:11

[107] Matthew 19:9

[108] Proverbs 13:4

[109] Revelation 21:4

[110] Hebrews 10:17

[111] Psalm 32:5

[112] Hebrews 10:23

[113] John 10:27-28

You are a shield around me, my glory, and the lifter of my head. I cry aloud to Yahweh, and He answers me from His holy hill. I lie down and sleep; I wake again, for He sustains me.[114] "Why are you cast down, O my soul, and why are you in turmoil within me? Hope in Him, for I shall again praise Him, my salvation, and my Father."[115] With the judgment you pronounce, you will be judged, and the measure you use will be measured to you.[116]

If you have faith and never doubt, you will not only do what has been done to the fig tree but even if you say to this mountain, 'Be taken up and cast into the sea,' it will be done.[117] One man gives freely yet grows all the richer; another withholds what he should give and only suffers want. Whoever brings blessings will be enriched, and the one who waters will himself be watered.[118] The fear of Yahweh is a fountain of life that one may turn away from the snares of death.[119]

Do not toil to acquire wealth; be discerning enough to desist. When your eyes light on it, it is gone, for suddenly it sprouts wings, flying like an eagle towards heaven.[120]

For even when we were with you, we gave you this command: If anyone is not willing to work, let him not eat. Some among you walk in idleness, not busy at work but busybodies. Now, we encourage and command you in Yahshua to work quietly and earn your own living. Do not grow weary in doing good.[121] Go to the ant, consider her ways, and be wise. Without having a chief, officer, or ruler, she prepares her bread in summer and gathers her food in harvest. How long will you lie there? When will you arise from your sleep? A little sleep, a little

---

[114] Psalm 3:3-5

[115] Psalm 42:5

[116] Matthew 7:2

[117] Matthew 21:21

[118] Proverbs 11:24-25

[119] Proverbs 14:27

[120] Proverbs 14:27

[121] 2 Thessalonians 3:10-13

slumber, a little folding of the hands to rest, and poverty will come upon you like a robber and want like an armed man.[122]

Love your enemies, bless those who curse you. Do good to those who hate you, and pray for those who persecute you.[123] See that no one repays anyone evil for evil but always seeks to do good to one another and to everyone.[124]

"The Pharisee, standing by himself, prayed, 'Yahweh, I thank You that I am not like other men—extortioners, unjust, adulterers, or even like this tax collector. I fast twice a week; I give tithes of all that I get.'"[125] But the thief comes only to steal, kill, and destroy. Yahshua came that we may have life and have it abundantly.[126]

"Watch and pray that you may not enter into temptation. The spirit is willing, but the flesh is weak."[127] Yahweh knows how to rescue the righteous from trials and to keep the unrighteous under punishment until the day of judgment.[128] I have stored up Your word in my heart that I might not sin against You.[129] Trust in Yahweh and do good. Dwell in the land and cultivate faithfulness. Delight yourself in Yahweh, and He will give you the desires of your heart.[130] He will bring forth your righteousness as the light and your justice as the noonday.[131]

Do not love the world or the things in it. If anyone loves the world, the love of Yahweh is not in him. For all that is in the world—the desires of the flesh, the desires of the eyes, and the pride of life—

---

[122] Proverbs 6:6-11

[123] Matthew 5:44

[124] 1 Thessalonians 5:15

[125] Luke 18:12

[126] John 10:10

[127] Matthew 26:41

[128] 2 Peter 2:9

[129] Psalms 119:11

[130] Psalms 27:3-4

[131] Psalms 37:6

is not from Yahweh but is from the world. The world is passing away along with its desires, but whoever does the will of Yahweh abides forever.[132]

Therefore, having put away falsehood, let each one of you speak the truth with his neighbor, for we are members of one another.[133] Truthful lips endure forever, but a lying tongue lasts only a moment.[134] A faithful witness does not lie, but a false witness breathes out lies.[135]

Blessed is the man who does not walk in the counsel of the wicked, or stand in the way of sinners, or sit in the seat of scoffers. But his delight is in the law of Yahweh, and on His law, he meditates day and night.[136] If sinners entice you, do not consent. If they say, "Come with us, let us lie in wait for blood; let us ambush the innocent without reason. Let us swallow them alive and whole, like those who go down to the pit. We shall find all kinds of precious goods; we shall fill our houses with plunder. Throw in your lot among us; we will all share the loot"—do not walk in their way. Hold back your foot from their path.[137]

Sexual immorality, all impurity, and covetousness must not even be named among you, as is proper among saints. Let there be no filthiness, foolish talk, or crude joking, which are out of place. Instead, let there be thanksgiving.[138] Abstain from sexual immorality; each one of you should know how to control your own body in holiness and honor in accordance with the will of Yahweh.[139] For all have sinned and fallen short of the glory of Yahweh.[140]

---

[132] 1 John 2:15-17

[133] Ephesians 4:25

[134] Proverbs 12:19

[135] Proverbs 14:15

[136] Psalms 1:1-2

[137] Proverbs 1:10-15

[138] Ephesians 5:3-4

[139] 1 Thessalonians 4:3-4

[140] Romans 3:23

Let the thief no longer steal, but rather let him labor, doing honest work with his own hands, so that he may have something to share with anyone in need.[141] The partner of a thief hates his own life; he hears the curse but discloses nothing.[142]

I have learned to be content in whatever situation I find myself. I know how to be brought low, and I know how to abound. In any and every circumstance, I have learned the secret of facing plenty and hunger, abundance and need.[143] Yahweh is a stronghold for the oppressed in times of trouble.[144]

Be watchful, and stand firm in your faith. Act with courage and be strong[145] as you wait for Yahshua. Be strong, and let your heart take courage as you wait for Yahshua.[146] No one who puts his hand to the plow and looks back is fit for the kingdom of Yahweh.[147]

I press on toward the prize of the upward call of Yahweh in Yahshua.[148].The one who endures to the end will be saved.[149] No unbelief made him waver concerning the promise of Yahweh. He grew strong in his faith as he gave glory to Yahweh, fully convinced that Yahweh was able to do what He had promised. His faith was counted to him as righteousness.[150]

Whoever hears my word and believes in Him who sent me has eternal life. He does not come into judgment but has passed from

---

[141] Ephesians 4:28

[142] Proverbs 29:24

[143] Philippians 4:11-12

[144] Psalms 9:9

[145] 1 Corinthians 16:13

[146] Psalms 27:14

[147] Luke 9:62

[148] Philippians 4:14

[149] Matthew 24:13

[150] Romans 4:2-22

death to life.[151] All that Yahweh gives me will come to me, and whoever comes to me, I will never cast out.[152]

Moreover, it is required of stewards that they be found faithful. [153] The earth is Yahweh's, and everything in it, the world, and those who dwell in it, for He has founded it upon the seas and established it upon the rivers.[154]

Finally, all of you have unity of mind, sympathy, brotherly love, a tender heart, and a humble mind. [155] Have mercy on those who doubt. [156] Yahweh is gracious and merciful, slow to anger, and abounding in steadfast love.[157] Be content with food and clothing.[158]

Be kind to one another, showing humility and gentleness, with patience, bearing with one another in love. Forgiving one another, as God in Christ forgave you.[159] The wisdom from above is first pure, then peaceable, gentle, open to reason, full of mercy and good fruits, impartial, and sincere.[160]

Put on the new self, created in the likeness of Yahweh, in true righteousness and holiness.[161] Ascribe to Yahweh the glory due to His name. Worship the splendor of His holiness; tremble before Him, all the earth. Worship![162]

---

[151] John 5:24

[152] John 6:37

[153] I Corinthians 4:2

[154] Psalms 24:1-2

[155] I Peter 3:8

[156] Jude 1:22

[157] Psalms 146:8

[158] I Timothy 6:8

[159] Ephesians 4:32

[160] James 3:17

[161] Ephesians 4:24

[162] Psalms 29:2

Holiness with contentment is a great gain.[163] "I am the vine; you are the branches." Whoever abides in Me and I in him bears much fruit; apart from Me, you can do nothing. [164] By this, Yahweh is glorified—that you bear much fruit, and so prove to be My disciples.[165]

For by grace, you have been saved through faith. This is not your own doing; it is the gift of Yahweh, not a result of works, so that no one may boast. We are His workmanship, created in Yahshua for good works, which Yahweh prepared beforehand, that we should walk in them,[166] walking in a manner worthy of Yahweh, fully pleasing to Him, bearing fruit in every good work, and increasing in the knowledge of Yahweh.[167]

Be attentive to My words; incline your ear to My sayings. Let them not escape from your sight; keep them within your heart. They are life to those who find them and healing to all their flesh.[168] Commit your work to Yahweh, and your plans will be established.[169]

Give thanks always and for everything to Yahweh in the name of Yahshua.[170] Enter His gates with thanksgiving and His courts with praise! Give thanks to Him and bless His name![171] Great peace has those who love Your law; nothing makes them stumble.[172]

Be submissive to rulers and authorities. Be obedient, ready for every good work.[173] Obey your leaders and submit to them, for they are keeping watch over your soul as those who will have to give an

---

[163] I Timothy 6:6

[164] John 15:5

[165] John 15:8

[166] Ephesians 2:8-10

[167] Colossians 1:10

[168] Proverbs 5:20-23

[169] Proverbs 16:3

[170] Ephesians 5:20

[171] Psalms 100:4

[172] Psalms 119:165

[173] Titus 3:1

account. Let them do this with joy and not with groaning, for that would be of no advantage to you.[174]

Do not join in with unbelievers. [175] Count it all joy, my brothers, when you meet trials of various kinds, knowing that the testing of your faith produces steadfastness. Let steadfastness have its full effect, that you may be perfect and complete, lacking in nothing. [176] I will lie down and sleep in peace, for You alone make me dwell in safety. [177] Continue steadfastly in prayer, being watchful in it with thanksgiving.[178] Pray without ceasing,[179] for the prayer of a righteous person has great power.[180]

Let no one despise your youth. Set an example for the believers in speech, in conduct, in love, in faith, and in purity.[181] Likewise, urge the younger men to be self-controlled. Show yourself in all respects to be a model of good works, and in your teaching, show integrity, dignity, and sound speech that cannot be condemned.[182]

Put away all filthiness and rampant wickedness and receive with meekness the implanted word, which is able to save our souls.[183] In your heart, honor Yahshua as holy, always being prepared to make a defense to anyone who asks for a reason for the hope that is in you. Do this with gentleness and respect.[184] The meek shall inherit the land and delight themselves in abundant peace.[185]

------

[174] Hebrews 13:17

[175] I Corinthians 6:14

[176] James 1:2

[177] Psalms 4:8

[178] Colossians 4:3

[179] I Thessalonians 5:17

[180] James 5:16

[181] I Timothy 4:12

[182] Titus 2:6

[183] James 1:21

[184] I Peter 3:14

[185] Psalms 31:11

Yahweh desires mercy, not sacrifice.[186] "I came not to call the righteous, but sinners." [187] He saved us, not because of works, according to his own mercy, but through the washing of regeneration and renewal by the Holy Spirit. [188] Let us, therefore, with confidence, draw near to the throne of grace that we may receive mercy and find grace to help in times of need.[189]

Remember not the sins of my youth or my transgressions. Remember me for the sake of Your goodness. [190] Let us be grateful for receiving a kingdom that cannot be shaken, and thus, let us offer to Him acceptable worship with reverence and awe.[191] The one who does not work but believes in Him who justifies the ungodly, his faith is counted as righteousness.[192] For our sake, He made Him who knew no sin to be sin, so that in Him, we might become the righteousness of Yahweh.[193] Let us be found in Him, not having a righteousness of our own that comes from the law, but that which comes through faith in Yahshua—the righteousness from Yahweh that depends on faith,[194] producing self-control, steadfastness, and holiness.[195]

"Rise and stand upon your feet, for I have appeared to you for this purpose, to appoint you as a servant and witness to the things in which you have seen Me and to those in which I will appear to you."[196]

Be a minister of Yahshua to the Gentiles in the priestly service of Yahweh's word so that the offering of the Gentiles may be acceptable

---

[186] Hosea 6:6

[187] Luke 5:32

[188] Titus 3:5

[189] Hebrews 4:16

[190] Psalms 25:7

[191] Hebrews 12:28

[192] Romans 4:5

[193] Romans 4:5

[194] Philippians 3:9

[195] 2 Peter 1:6-7

[196] Acts 26:16

and sanctified by the Holy Spirit.[197] Let each of you look not only to his own interests but also to the interests of others.[198] As each has received a gift, use it to serve one another as good stewards of Yahweh's varied grace.[199]

"When they deliver you over, do not be anxious about how you are to speak or what you are to say, for what you are to say will be given to you in that hour. It is not you who speak, but the Spirit of Yahweh speaking through you."[200]

The fruit of the righteous is a tree of life,[201] and whoever captures souls is wise.[202] The aim of our charge is love that comes from a pure heart, a good conscience, and sincere faith[203] so that you may approve what is excellent and be pure and blameless for the day of Yahshua.[204] Having purified your souls by obedience to the truth, show sincere brotherly love, loving one another earnestly from a pure heart.[205]

If you indeed continue in the faith, stable and steadfast, not shifting from the hope of the gospel that you heard, which has been proclaimed in all creation under heaven, you will be reconciled.[206] A slack hand causes poverty, but the hand of the diligent makes rich.[207] I am sure of this: He who began a good work in you will bring it to

---

[197] Romans 15:16

[198] Philippians 2:4

[199] I Peter 4:10

[200] Matthew 10:19-20

[201] Proverbs 12:30

[202] Proverbs 11:30

[203] I Timothy 1:15

[204] Philippians 1:10

[205] I Peter 1:22

[206] Colossians 1:22

[207] Proverbs 10:4

completion on the day of Yahshua.[208] It is better to take refuge in Yahweh than to trust in man.[209]

Lead me in Your truth and teach me, for You are the Father of my salvation,[210] merciful and gracious, slow to anger.[211]

Everyone born of Yahweh overcomes the world through faith. [212] All who practice the fear of Yahweh gain true understanding, and His praise endures forever![213] Let the wise listen and increase in learning, and let those with understanding seek guidance. [214] Yahweh grants wisdom: from His mouth come knowledge and understanding. He stores up sound wisdom for the upright and is a shield to those who walk in integrity.[215] Without counsel, plans fail, but with many advisers, they succeed.[216]

"The hour is coming and is now here when true worshipers will worship Yahweh in spirit and truth, for Yahweh is seeking such people to worship Him.[217] Come, let us worship and bow down; let us kneel before Yahweh."[218]

Admit when you are troubled. Stay honest with yourself. Speak with others and heal those you've harmed. Carry the message without expecting a reward, and pray to Yahweh through Yahshua by the Spirit. Admitting problems can feel like losing power, but believe that Yahweh can restore sanity. Decide to turn your life over to Him.

---

[208] Philippians 1:6

[209] Psalms 118:8

[210] Psalms 25:5

[211] Psalm 103:8

[212] I John 5:4

[213] Psalms 111:10

[214] Proverbs 1:5

[215] Proverbs 2:6-7

[216] Proverbs 15:22

[217] John 4:23

[218] Psalms 95:6

Examine your fears and face them, for we must recognize that human beings are prone to sin.

Be prepared for Yahweh to remove your defects. Humbly ask Him to take away your shortcomings. Make peace with everyone you have ever harmed, seeking direct reconciliation, except when doing so would cause further injury. And always admit when you are wrong.

***

- **Strength:** Yahweh brings healing into our lives through our weaknesses. In our journey of recovery, we discover that true strength lies in acknowledging our powerlessness.

- **Honor:** In his plan, honor is something we seek, but honor is received through humility, for this is the true path to honor.

- **Love:** He designed us for connection and relationship. Through trust, we can experience true love.

- **Growth:** His way is not easy. Without a willingness to follow His plan, we limit our growth. We need an open heart to have His will of growth.

- **Fulfillment:** His ways are mysterious and not like our ways. Sacrifice and sharing with others is the true path of fulfillment.

- **Hope:** Struggles and trials are part of the journey, but hope does not disappoint. We must endure hardships in faith, knowing that He loves us.

- **Victory:** To truly surrender ourselves is how life begins, His will for us to come to Him and be victorious.

- **Reward:** We are His hands, feet, and mouth. In being faithful, we gain peace and satisfaction and are obedient to Him.

- **Free:** Holding grudges brings bondage to the one not forgiven. We must forgive others, just as we were forgiven.

- **Healing:** Healing begins when we confess our shortcomings and failures to Him and to those we have failed.

- **Closure:** Restitution isn't always financial; it can be emotional or related to non-material issues we experience closure through.

- **Security:** In all things, we must take responsibility for our actions. This means not blaming others or expecting someone else to carry our burdens. We experience security when we fulfill our responsibilities, admit our mistakes, and do our part each day.

6

Appreciation of The Gospel

On the path of righteousness, every word you speak must be lived out in your actions. Your words should align with your deeds, for this is why faith without works is dead.

True faith is reflected through action, love, sacrifice, strength, and commitment to what has been proclaimed. By applying all the principles shared in this book, your life will be filled with many blessings. Through this journey, much will be revealed and manifested.

In life, twelve attributes are gained: hope, power, character, clarity, security, abundance, wisdom, freedom, self-control, happiness, serenity, and, above all, peace.

<u>Relationships and Love</u>

- **Appreciation**: You respect and value your partner and express gratitude often.

- **Commitment**: You are invested in your partner and the relationship; you give the relationship adequate time and energy.

- **Conflict Resolution:** You take responsibility for your actions and work as a team to solve problems.

- **Empathy**: You take your partner's perspective and understand their feelings, even if you do not always agree.

- **Independence:** You have your own interests and goals separate from your partner's.

- **Safety:** You respect your partner's boundaries. You feel safe physically, intellectually, and emotionally.

- **Balance:** You find happiness in time spent together and apart. Some needs are met outside the relationship (friends, hobbies, etc.).

- **Commonality**: You share important goals, beliefs, and values together.

- **Effective Communication:** You communicate your own needs and wishes while respecting those of your partner.

- **Honesty:** Your actions align with your words. The thoughts and feelings you express are genuine. Intimacy- You feel close and connected with your partner physically and emotionally.

- **Self-Confidence:** You feel comfortable being yourself in a relationship.

Couples usually express appreciation through healthy relationships associated with physical and mental wellness. Love languages are the ways people show and receive love. By learning your partner's love language and helping them learn yours, you will be better at sharing positive feelings.

- **Acts of Service**: Complete chores, caring for children, working to provide for the family, and other beneficial tasks.

- **Gifts**: Giving presents, buying flowers, creating something for your partner, and other thoughtful surprises.

- **Physical Touch**: Holding hands, spending intimate time, cuddling, and affection.

- **Quality Time**: Sharing meals, having conversations, going on a date, and being present with your partner.

- **Words of Affirmation**: Stating feelings, giving encouragement, giving compliments, sharing positive thoughts.

Incarceration:

Unless you are an incarcerated person, you cannot have a full understanding of what it means to be alone. It is very hard inside. People need help with loneliness and want some attention. Trying to get by on what the system provides only creates room for wanting more and can lead to feeling empty. This can lead to getting into relationships for the wrong reasons to fill voids—such as money, gifts, food, visits, and loneliness. Most of these feelings can be momentary. A true relationship should be grounded in mutual desires rather than transient needs.

Yahweh should be our first priority, then others. "It is not good for man to be alone. Let's make him a helper in our image."[219] He assures our happiness, and relying on others to fulfill our needs can sometimes lead to a sense of being used, which can diminish self-esteem and lower expectations. We were created to benefit one another, not to exploit each other.

The first step toward compassion is learning to be content with solitude. A healthy relationship with another person is important, but within Yahweh, we are never truly alone. Many have found that placing their trust in Yahweh has helped them improve their lives, even after reaching the brink of despair. By integrating Yahweh into everything you say, think, feel, and do, you reveal who you truly are and what you have become. This message resonates both within society and among those who have faced incarceration.

If you meet someone special, you first must be where you're needed within Yahweh. Prayer is the most helpful thing to do. Prayer can guide you anywhere you desire, even when praying for two opposite things; eventually, they can be attacked by the accuser/adversary.

---

[219] Genesis 2:18

Prayer requires being selfless, humble, offering, and loving. We must give as much as we receive to show love; nobody likes to feel used or lied to. Selfishness is lying, using, or manipulating people to gain, whereas selflessness is trust, respect, and loyalty through righteousness.

Being strong for your special someone in society as well as yourself builds strength mentally and physically. Being incarcerated doesn't change wanting someone in society, and visits provide crucial opportunities for meaningful interaction.

Prayer comes with things hoped for; it is your special someone who has to be able to have patience and want a relationship or companion inside. Differences have to be settled as situations come and go each time; you must call upon Yahweh for guidance. Marriage is sometimes sought out, as well as unity, formalization, and sanctification of union with one another. Together and with Yahweh, unity, and friendship must be nurtured through mutual understanding and trust, knowing your spouse as Yahweh does in marriage.

Marriage is an ordained covenant between Yahweh and spouses designed for the partners to respect each other, the husband to be sensitive, and to love one another. Together, blessings are to be received through grace and guidance. It can be hard and painful; it requires being vulnerable, resolving conflicts, and being confronted with the truth, even when it hurts, by working through difficulties in maturity.

Being able to put your spouse first is the first step in the union. Next, both spouses need to be able to devote themselves to knowing and learning all possible about one another. Strengths need to be the focus while Yahweh works on weaknesses and healing; you must be willing to go above and beyond and make every effort in unity, selflessness, and humbleness.

Spiritual men and women serve as exemplars of diligence, love, and devotion to Yahshua. Their lives lay a path for others to follow daily, guiding them toward a deeper union with Him. We, the body of people that make up a church, need to be in complete obedience to Yahweh and for His plans to work through Christ within us.

Husbands are the head of their wives as Yahshua is the head of the body of people (the Church) and our Savior. Honor Yahshua as the head of the church; he is an example to others who witness how we should be as a body in unity and prayer. To marry while incarcerated, you will need the following documents and information: your name and inmate number, a letter of intent to marry, and the name, address, and phone number of your intended spouse. Additionally, you will need a marriage license, social security card, ID, wedding bands, and a birth certificate. You will also require two to five witnesses to complete the process.

Marriage is a sacred gift to be cherished and respected. It is not for those who enter into it without proper preparation or who act irresponsibly. Marriage is a permanent commitment designed by Yahweh to be a source of fruitfulness and blessing in our lives. We must approach it one day at a time, evolving from a relationship to a partnership and from a couple to a companionship. Marriage should be selfless, focusing on the needs of your spouse, and should be rooted in love and respect. By nurturing confidence through both words and actions, we honor this divine gift.

In prison, to accomplish or establish a great marriage, praying together by phone or Jpay (email), letters and visits is important. You need to be thankful for the smallest things– trials, joy, communication, and even scripture to help in the tough times, especially loneliness. Be honest with your spouse, vent, listen, care for needs, care for stress, care for safety, and pray through worries. It is a decision made to build with your spouse; it can create a strong bond beyond our greatest imagination/ expectations.

Men and women were created to be loved by Yahweh and one another as He created someone for everyone and everything. Although it may not always be easy, it can be satisfying, joyful, and loving when both parties love one another, no matter the circumstances. The best type of marriage is one kept between spouses, keeps full disclosure, focuses on one another, never adds other's failures, is trustworthy and secure. The goal is to remain through hard times, trials, and mistakes. Shifting blame, being selfish, and becoming weak can be replaced with being excited, joyful, loving, and very heartfelt. Patience is a requirement for getting to know your spouse better and having a joyful and fun marriage; allowing Yahweh to guide of the journey and being thankful allows abundant blessings to walk in His covenant in heaven for all eternity.

Prayer, love, patience, support, encouragement, and faith in Yahweh help when in prison. He can give you the peace you need to enjoy life together despite the circumstances through Holy Matrimony. A relationship built on a foundation of trust, respect, and joy will cause satisfaction in what we have through love, peace, joy, companionship, trust, loyalty, and a nourishing relationship. With Him in the center of marriage, every battle, victory, good or bad day, day in prison or out, and every gift belongs to Yahweh.

Marriage is a lifetime commitment by the faith and hope of Yahweh's truth. We are to be confident in what we hope for and secure of what we can't see. We must have a desire for certain expectations and place our hope in Him as He works in us through our spirit by prayer, communication, understanding, teachings, and love. We are to have faith that we are placed with who we belong and where we belong within their hearts and lives. We are meant to work together as a team to glorify Yahweh by living a righteous life so we can reach heaven; he has a purpose for marriage through Yahshua, even for prisoners.

Both spouses are responsible for the family, working or managing the home, and attending service. Aches and joys are felt, decisions are made together, finances are handled together, sickness, depression, and loneliness are felt even celebration is felt by spouses. We must treat one another as His gift to enjoy His blessings every day; vows must be taken seriously, as our goal should be to get to Heaven. Even though we are created as two individuals with different likes, hurts, fears wants, and needs, we are called to be one mind, body, and spirit in Yahshua to be completed. We must love properly, which comes in the form of patience, love, kindness, and truth. We are not to envy, boast, be proud, dishonor, self-seek, angry, or keep a record of bad only to protect, trust, hope, and preserve, because love must never fail; we are blessed through Yahshua.

Discussing our lives helps us to stay on the same page by listening to one another's options and factors and being considerate to help our spouse feel normal and included; this shows respect. A listening ear is always helpful in needing advice or releasing stress. Listening involves not being selfish, knowing it's not about you at the time, keeping a positive attitude, being patient, and showing respect.

Our spouses always want to feel needed and included in our lives, so we must do so with everything; we must love our spouses even when they don't deserve it or seem to be unlovable. Our love must be unconditional and very sincere. It must be peaceful so that the right decisions and choices can be made together. Trust, honesty, and faithfulness are part of who we are in Yahshua; Yahshua must be number one.

If you don't move on from past hurts, deceit takes root, mistrust becomes your reality, and doubts dominate your thoughts—these are forces of darkness. However, the forces of light enable you to forgive those who have wronged you and those you have wronged, allowing healing to bring peace. Living in trust, honesty, and faithfulness through scripture serves as a guide in marriage. Prayer is essential to any marriage. It builds relationships, connects hearts, and draws us closer to Yahshua. Through prayer, we can be open and honest, communicate our needs, seek direction, and strengthen our bond.

Confessing our sins and repenting through communication brings freedom and helps us grow closer to our spouses, evolving our marriage. Family prayer is crucial, as it encourages others to seek Yahshua. Taking communion, along with prayer and meditation, deepens the blessings in our lives. These acts of faith allow Yahshua's power to work in us and through us, as prayer has the power to change everything.

There are several scriptures to guide spouses through marriage:

- Genesis 2:18

- Matthew 19:26

- Hebrews 11:1

- Romans 8:28

- Philippians 4:11

- Genesis 2:24

- 1 Corinthians 12:27

- Ephesians 5:22-33

- 1Peter 3:7

- Romans 12:9-10

- Proverbs 3:5

- Proverbs 12:17

- Matthew 18:20

- 1 Thessalonians 5:17

- 2 Corinthians 5:7

- Matthew 6:34

Yahweh is always listening to us. He loves to hear our prayers, and we should love to praise Yahweh and thank Him for our blessings.

I have been in many relationships, but only two engagements where marriage was the plan. Over time, mixed feelings would develop—joy, peace, love, spiritual wellness, and happiness, but also insecurities, loneliness, financial struggles, disappointment, and emotional stress. Learning how to be strong through these situations requires faith. Staying strong in prison isn't easy, but we must first rely on Yahweh for strength. Only then can we lean on extended and immediate family for additional support as we build on a solid foundation. For many, they only have themselves to rely on.

Though circumstances may be difficult, joy should come from Yahweh. There are also programs that can reduce sentences, hobbies to enjoy, spiritual and emotional support, and visits available. A strong support system can help us overcome negativity. As tough times pass, we can rise above challenges with lightheartedness and genuine love.

During these trials, we must be specific and truthful about our circumstances, striving to rise above others' thoughts and expectations. We must thank Yahweh for what we have and continue to hope for what is to come. Along this journey, not everyone will stick around as you thought they would. Many personal problems will eventually cause some to drift away. Some may stay in touch through JPay email or phone calls, but it can be deeply painful when others don't fully understand your situation. We need family, spouses, partners, and companions to help us endure prison. Through Yahshua, we must find peace and joy in our hearts. To overcome the destruction of the prison, we must live righteously, keeping a strong and positive mind to navigate and rise above our shortcomings.

Much prayer is needed—both together and individually. It is much harder without visits or a solid support system. Listening to each other is crucial to keeping your family together throughout your prison experience. This will not be an easy task if you and your family aren't aligned in positivity and faith.

As my dreams manifest into reality before my eyes, the partner meant for me will be revealed. I radiate beauty, charm, and grace. Each day, I am in control of my illnesses. Obstacles are clearing out of my path, and greatness is being carved. I wake up each day with strength in my heart and clarity in my mind. My fears of tomorrow melt away.

I am at peace with all that has happened, all that is happening, and all that will happen. My nature is divine; I am a spiritual being, and my life is just beginning. I am the stepping stone and the poet, the architect of my life, building its foundation and choosing its content.

I am superior to negative thoughts and low actions. I use the talents Yahweh has given me, replacing anger with love. I possess the qualities needed to be successful. Creative energy surges through me, leading me to new and brilliant ideas. Happiness is a choice. My ability to conquer challenges is limitless, my potential for success is infinite, and my time, effort, and ideas are worthy of reward.

I am courageous; my thoughts are filled with positivity, and my life overflows with prosperity. I abandon old habits and embrace new, more positive ones. Many people look up to me and recognize my worth. I am admired and blessed with an incredible support system, including my five children and family. I acknowledge my own self-worth, and my confidence soars as I understand that everything happening is for my ultimate good. I am a powerhouse; I am indestructible. Though these times are difficult, they are but a short phase of my life.

My future is the ideal projection of what I envision now. I speak and repeat these affirmations to uplift and encourage myself, knowing that Yahweh guides me. I love and approve of myself. Though I may not fully understand the good in this situation, I know it is present. I choose to look at things with hope and optimism. I seek help and guidance when needed, and I refuse to give up because I now understand compassion.

I feel the love that isn't physically present. I forgive myself for past mistakes, and I accept that anger once harmed my life. I offer an apology to those affected by the anger I once knew, and I forgive!

7

Second Chances

We live in a world filled with conflict, where grief, hurt, and brokenness often turn into anger and its many forms. Like many today, we may find ourselves discouraged by grief and anger, causing us to stray from faith and seek comfort in familiar but misguided places. We must remember that as individuals, couples, families, and as the church—the body of believers— Yahweh is our builder and redeemer. Yahweh offers us hope. As the world changes, we too can change, but Yahweh remains the same today, yesterday, and forever. In His truth, we are renewed.

As human beings, we often seek safety in the wrong places, clinging to the culture and traditions that are familiar to us. Our lives, both within the church and outside of it, must be equally rooted in confidence in Yahweh. We need to stop living in fear of what is to come and instead trust that in the present, we are safe in Yahweh through His Word. When we pray, we should pray as one, placing our confidence in Yahweh. Through the power of His truth and communication, He can transform our lives. We need Yahweh to awaken us to reality so we can thank Him for every moment of life.

We live in a world of diminished potential, decline, and destruction. It often surprises us when life doesn't unfold as we imagined. Too often, we live in delusion rather than reality. Yahweh created the world to be perfect, a place of paradise, but we fall short of that potential. We were created to be much more, to do much more, yet human nature leads us to decline. This diminished potential often ends in destruction.

When Yahweh created Adam from the dust of the earth and breathed life into him, He called all creation—humans and all living creatures—good. We were meant to be revealed as children of Yahweh, liberated from bondage and decay. However, because of

Adam and Eve's disobedience, we now live in a world marred by sin. Without Yahweh's touch, marriages, families, and spiritual wellness cannot endure.

In the beginning, we experience new birth, new beginnings, and new creation, but when we lose sight of Yahweh's promises and refuse to work for Him, we risk falling into decline. Without rescue, redemption, healing, and faith, we suffer diminished potential by our very human nature. Yahweh controls the universe and where it goes, but He gave us free will, and it is our decisions and choices that determine if we accept or decline Yahweh. Trust in the world includes loss of light, power, promise, and hope. Trust in the supernatural gains--because light gains power, promise, and hope through Yahweh's control.

In a tomb, Yahshua lay dead; out of that same tomb, he walked. Yahweh does his work not one time but many times. In our lives, church, nation, and world, Yahweh can build marriages and churches and redo and rework both today and tomorrow; it only allows our trust. He will send the Holy Spirit to teach us a better way through strength and weaknesses, no matter our rage, discouragement, decay, and hopelessness. He is a builder and redirector of strength.

We must embrace the good with the bad. No matter the conditions, we have to believe and have hope in Yahweh.

Having faith allows us to rebuild, confessing sins and falling short in our individual lives as marriages and families build. Until we instill this in our churches and nations, we can't experience the rebuilding process. Encouragement to read scripture, confession, and worship needs to be tough to rebuild. We must not let rage, anger, bitterness, dismay, or grief control us but replace it with rescue, renewal, and restoration from Yahweh as He awaits our acceptance.

The pattern of this world is living below Yahweh's given potential. We must ascend to paradise and redemption, allowing transformation within the renewing of our minds. A new beginning is given a new life once we fully trust Yahweh, allowing the change to manifest within us into heaven. Death by baptism and death by spirit raise us to a new life in paradise. We then can show love, passion, and goodness and can bring a cherished marriage and children who love us and trust us. The pattern was broken on the cross by Yahshua, the resurrection from the tomb, and the renewing. Understanding brokenness and sinful nature turns old ways into His new ways; declare with your mouth, believe with your heart, call on His name, and return to Him by faith.

Can you show you are a new creation to a spouse, children, coworkers, friends, or associates? Are you singing hope or living in despair of humanity?

Be the person who sings of hope by experiencing Yahweh and becoming His new creation—a testimony for others to witness. Do not remain the old person trapped in despair. Instead of offering yourself to sin and facing eternal fire and brimstone, offer yourself to righteousness so you may inherit eternal life filled with milk, honey, and peace. Too often, we have been taught to grieve in the wrong places, clinging to things that lead to bondage and decay. But we must return to the celebration of Yahweh's will—not seeking what we want from Him but surrendering to the origins of His divine purpose for creation.

Only Yahweh can break the cycle of decline, destruction, and death brought on by sin. We must believe that through Yahshua, we have walked out of the tomb resurrected given a second chance at a new beginning. Through faith and trust in Him, we can be saved. This is the true path to redemption.

I was a believer in a fresh start before incarceration. During incarceration, I've been striving to rise above my mistakes and the circumstances of them, concentrating on rehabilitation and working towards returning home to my family and support system. I would like clarity to be seen in taking responsibility and working towards change. Though I intended no harm physically, mentally, or emotionally, I still committed a crime. I have repented, and I hope for forgiveness, mercy, grace, and favor to be shown because I am not a murderer or a bad person. I had no joy in my actions. They have caused many nights of sorrow and pain. But on my journey, I aim to be cautious of what's said, done, and thought of and to be thought of as who I am, not who I was in the past at the beginning of my journey, but my who I am now on my path to peace and unity.

In continuing my journey, I have earned certificates and have been working on my behaviors and actions, because my file in prison will determine whether I am released back into society. With this awareness, I approach my future with greater insight, recognizing that my choices and decisions must be positive. Through the programs I've participated in and the reading material I've studied, I've gained valuable tactics for self-improvement, preparing to reenter society as a better person.

Failure is not final, and delays are not setbacks. Yahweh uses those who have stumbled and made poor choices—they are still worthy of His grace. Carnal thinking tells us that once a failure, always a failure. But spiritual thinking reminds us that even when we fail, we can be empowered by Yahweh. No matter the failure—whether as a spouse, parent, friend, or leader—we all fall short at times.

Simon, who later became Peter, gave up his vocation, was sincere and committed, and had a big heart, yet he also failed. Yahweh lifted him up repeatedly, gave him a voice, and chose him as one of His first representatives and followers. There is not a person named in the Bible who didn't fail Yahweh. Yet, through failure, we access His promises and learn to become better. No one can love, worship, or praise Yahweh any better because of their failures. We are not dismissed, isolated, or hidden away because of our mistakes. Instead, Yahweh picks us up, calls us to stand, and equips us to be leaders for Him. Just as Simon's failures were revealed, as Peter he grew from stumbling to walking in faith.

We must not allow failure to defeat or discourage us, leading us to live in despair and darkness when we don't have to. We often ask,

"Why?" But Yahweh knew we would fail. We may be surprised by our failures, but Yahweh is not. Failure is part of His plan to draw us closer to Him and make us better.

When we fail, we often believe we can hide from Yahweh. We run away, close ourselves off, and feel as if He is disappointed in us. But the truth is, He loves us despite our failures. He loves us in the very face of our failures. Yahshua lived the life we couldn't, died the death we deserved, and rose again so that we could receive the love and forgiveness we don't deserve.

Even when we feel unloved, we are watched over and prayed for. Too often, we pray for those who are already doing well, neglecting those who need help to improve. If we are to reflect the image of Yahweh, we must pray for everyone, whether they are failing or succeeding. Arrogance often leads to failure, but Yahweh has a plan in place for our shortcomings.

As we are strengthened, we are called to strengthen others through prayer and action. By doing so, we can help save those who believe in Yahshua, as He intercedes for us with Yahweh. Yahweh doesn't count our failures—He counts our victories. He values not our outward appearance but our hearts. We must look beyond our failures to the light of our future. When we pray over our failures, Yahweh's plans for us can manifest, and we begin to see ourselves through His eyes.

Failure is only final when we refuse Yahweh's help. We were created to depend on Him and one another, not to be independent of Him or others. We must assist the poor, the hurt, and the brokenhearted. In the eyes of society, we may be seen as prisoners of our past failures, but failure is only final if we allow our faith to be broken through brokenness. We must humble ourselves and hold on to our faith in Yahweh.

Do your failures haunt you? What weighs you down? Have you failed in relationships, marriage, children, character, hatred, greed, dishonesty, or sexual immortality? Have you been worshipping or loving Yahweh? Have you forgiven others?

Whatever the failing, Yahweh forgives you; don't hide behind your failures as if Yahweh can't see them. Once failure is confessed, we are purified from unrighteousness. Yahweh is the only one who can remove past failures and mistakes from existence. So, trust in Him, don't view what's been given, and focus only on transformation, cleansing, and forgiveness. We are, by human nature, failures and can't get past those failures alone. But the moment Yahshua died by his crucifixion and was resurrected, we were forgiven and made new by the blood He shed. So, give Him your sin and take the Word and trust in him. Serve others as instructed, consume the promises, enjoy life and live without guilt, and share his faith and hope with the world. We must take communion to keep the covenant made between us and Yahweh, as the bread represents the body of Yahshua, the wine represents his blood, and the Word represents the truth and promise.

Communion is a declaration of who we are within Yahweh and who we are with Yahshua. It's the celebration of what we've done by faith to open ourselves up to a new life. Failure no longer defines us, but forgiveness does. Our hope gives us joy; we no longer have to live in bondage or be weighed down by the darkness that comes from failure. We can now live in celebration of the hope for the Lamb of Yahweh. We must gain wisdom, maturity, and knowledge from the Word.

I had to be taught how to treat a family and how to make proper decisions and choices that would make life better. I was inexperienced in Yahweh's word but had little experience in the world. I had my children out of wedlock. Having children is a major sacrifice for a woman to make. I did my best to support my children's mothers. I still do my best, although we are apart. I received the guidance later; the wisdom gene was missing, and lessons needed to be taught and learned. I began to pray, which led to learning and growing. As a toddler, I was never shown the proper way to do things, and it stuck with me through life. I had to learn through experience. As a child, I didn't understand the power or importance of spirituality. In my teenage and adult years, I was double-minded until I began my full walk with the Lord. It was time for me to decide: *Will my choices hurt, damage, or accomplish anything?* I had to decide what to live for and what was important. I had to gain wisdom, understanding, and knowledge. I had to let go of the carnal for the spiritual. I am still a work in progress, but I have come a long way. I am anointed.

Solomon was asked by Yahweh what his greatest desire was, and he asked for wisdom. As a king, Solomon knew he needed to be better than his father, David, who led differently than he did. Through wisdom, Solomon gained life, prosperity, and power. He became one of Israel's greatest kings, known for his accomplishments, wealth, and influence. In his era, he was one of the richest men on earth. Wisdom is the ability to see, think, and hear from Yahweh's perspective, no matter what life throws your way. Responding appropriately with wisdom leads to better outcomes rather than pursuing temporary, selfish ambitions. Wisdom guides us in the choices we make each day, aligning us with Yahweh's view. We need Yahweh's insight to seek the right information and knowledge. Wisdom is a gift from Yahweh, meant to be applied to the right circumstances in life for our benefit, depending on how earnestly we seek His guidance.

Regardless of age or experience, we all need wisdom. It brings maturity and helps us consistently make good choices. Wisdom is not something we are born with; it must be sought within our hearts. It helps us view things differently, prevents us from making foolish choices, protects us from wickedness, keeps us from perverse speech, and saves us from walking the path of darkness. Wisdom helps us build a strong foundation in life, guiding us to walk and run with purpose rather than stumble and fall. In a world dominated by despair, wisdom brings hope. We all have priorities, whether we write them down or not. Many of us avoid writing them down because we don't want to be held accountable. However, making wisdom a priority can profoundly impact our lives, as it helps us understand that our choices and decisions affect more than just ourselves.

Communication is another area where wisdom is essential. "A gentle answer turns away wrath, but a harsh word stirs up anger."[220] Generosity is also vital: "Honor Yahweh with your wealth."[221] To experience true prosperity, we must not only pray but live a life of prosperity through prayer. With pride comes disgrace, but with humility comes wisdom. Pride convinces us that we need no one else and that our truth alone matters. Humility, however, acknowledges our need for others and the truth of Yahweh. Transforming our prayers from requests for worldly things into prayers for wisdom and a deeper reliance on Yahweh is crucial: "The fear of Yahweh is the beginning of wisdom, and knowledge of the Holy Spirit is understanding."[222] We must put our faith in Yahshua's name for a life of perfection, the death of sins, the healing of our imperfections, and His resurrection for new life to receive wisdom.

Self-control is one aspect of the fruit of the Spirit, and it is essential for growing in maturity, especially as a parent and father. Children will always remember when change comes into your lives. As we follow Yahweh, our children will have a worthy example of a solid foundation built on love and wisdom. Children want to know that they make us proud and that we love them. They search for their identity, understand who they are, and find security within their families. Children look to their parents to be taught properly. In today's society, it is rare to find a father who faithfully stands by his wife, but dads are the strength families need. Integrity must be displayed in difficult times, situations, and circumstances to endure and lift up those who are weak, including our children. Integrity is what distinguishes great leaders in the home. Men of strength and integrity are needed, as we

---

[220] Proverbs 15:1
[221] Proverbs 3:9
[222] Proverbs 9:10

want our children to follow us, just as Yahweh wants us to follow Him. This is how we are blessed in righteousness.

I want my son to be better than I was. I would start with things I was never shown, how to accomplish things I didn't accomplish, and lead as great as I have or even greater. A dad is a man of integrity, love, and leadership. We can learn this from our Heavenly Father Yahweh, The Maker of men and The Maker of the world. We must receive His message; it disciplines and instructs. Fatherhood is a gift given to us by Yahweh. It requires responsibility and opportunity to teach, love, nurture, and grow. It is the first line of ministry, along with ministering to our wives, partners, and spouses. It can take place in homes, by phone, in our streets, at our place of fellowship, or anywhere of our choosing. Our role as fathers never end because a good father is the most honorable and trustworthy way to show our children that we love them, and we are to show them by example the ways of Yahweh as called.

The material doesn't define how our children will remember us; it is by conversation, visiting, and encouragement. Children remember cooked meals, talks, bedtime stories, riding bikes, and the time spent trying to lead and counsel them. We can get everything accomplished through Yahweh; we are still going to struggle and fail, but Yahweh already knew. The promise is to never struggle alone. We must seek Yahweh and fellowship with our brothers and sisters of faith. We must share our struggles, pray regularly, and admit our mistakes, not just to one another but also to Yahweh. Children even need apologies sometimes and to be asked to forgive us throughout our mistakes. Lack of faith allows our children to be pregnant girls and criminal boys and imprisoned minors.

Fathers are important because Yahweh is important to us. A child's connection to us is normally their connection with Yahweh, so we need to remain in bond. The potential impact of a good child and Godly child is they need to have their dad present, the same as their mom. It's greater to be a learning parent than an absent dad.

Fatherhood influences how a child lives, and the next generation's value on sin and righteousness in behavior. Spending even just an hour at home with our children can leave a legacy of good character, love, and support. When we show our children love, they feel protected and secure. This helps prevent them from seeking love and acceptance outside the home, steering them away from dangerous influences like gangs or premarital sex. When they know their identity and feel valued, they won't feel the need to fit in elsewhere. Even nonspiritual people understand the importance of fathers loving their children. Strong fathers are essential and deserve recognition, encouragement, and praise. Children who know they are loved and cared for are emotionally secure and stable.

Loving, present fathers contribute to lower rates of depression in children, increased security in their surroundings, less behavioral trouble, and better social skills. When fathers are involved, there are lower levels of violence, greater respect for both men and women and stronger self-worth. For girls, this involvement can mean protection from seeking approval and love through harmful means, such as early sexual activity, which in turn can prevent early pregnancies. The impact of a loving father resonates far into the future, influencing their children's lives in profound ways.

As scripture tells us, love is the greatest of all values, even surpassing hope and faith. The highest form of love is *agape*—Yahweh's self-sacrificial love that extends to both friends and enemies. This is the love we can also give to our children. Agape love is unconditional, selfless, and sacrificial—the same love Yahweh displayed through Yahshua's total commitment to us, even when we didn't deserve or seek it. This love is most powerfully demonstrated when one person has much to give to another who is in need. Our children need to hear us say we love them, but more importantly, they need to see it in our actions. Love must be experienced to be understood.

To truly give love, we must first receive it from Yahweh and then allow it to flow through us as we follow His example. Yahweh's love is shown through patience, kindness, discipline, forgiveness, and security. We can give without loving, but we cannot love without giving. Yahweh gives us His time, His security, and His peace.

Patient love listens intently, even during simple conversations with our children. It teaches them to do things on their own without us always needing to be present. Patient love is about teaching important lessons over time without getting angry when our children don't get things right immediately. It's about laying down our own desires for Yahweh's sake and changing how we relate to our children. Kind love goes out of its way to benefit others. It's shown in giving compliments, expressing pride through words, playing with our children instead of just watching, and spending time with them, like going out to dinner.

Disciplined love prepares our children for the future. It protects, blesses, and corrects them, helping them respect others, follow the rules, and understand boundaries and values. Proper discipline does not discourage children or provoke them to anger. We should not let our emotions drive negative actions when disciplining our children. It is unwise to push them to the breaking point or yell at them just because that was done to us. Instead, we should encourage them, even when correcting their behavior. Children pick up on what is acceptable and what is not, and they learn that behaving well is a blessing that pleases their parents. As a result, their behavior improves, and the more we guide them with love, the more they will grow in respect and love for us as parents.

A lack of involvement or discipline can incite anger in a child even more than harsh discipline. The more involved we are in our children's lives, the less likely they are to become bitter or angry. Fathers who lead with love, discipline, and kindness shape the next generation to walk in righteousness.

Taking time to correctly discipline our children instead of avoiding them or neglecting them, we can communicate through prison conversation or by visits, letters, or phone. This can help establish acceptance and show how proper things should be done in our homes. Family discipline begins with the standards. We talk with our children about unacceptable behavior and always praying. If disobedience occurs the level of discipline should be increased. Discipline should be worked out by both fathers and mothers so that children receive a consistent understanding of behavior at home.

Forgiving is love. We must forgive whoever has wronged us, whether our children or family. Bitterness between people is rotten; the best thing to do is settle things positively by grace. Grace is an underserved favor. Yahshua took our punishment for us to receive pardon, being forgiven for all the wrongs we didn't earn or deserve. Once we receive forgiveness, we can then forgive others even when they don't deserve it; Yahshua's grace removes bitterness from our hearts no matter how long it is held. Realizing how much Yahweh forgives us helps it to be easier to forgive others.

Bitterness and frustration build from struggle and past actions of hurt, but peace gives us the opportunity to heal and have positive involvement.

I've asked my children to forgive me for my absence, and I pray for them and for me to always be known as a great father. In doing so, I hope to pass on my legacy down generations, and that enough was learned to build a strong foundation of love. Fathers are responsible for the instruction of their children. We are the ones who teach them how to make decisions. Although, as a baby, the mother teaches the child the basics of right and wrong, by puberty, the father teaches the child the responsibility to make decisions and the consequences of them.

The unity of the mother's and father's law and instructions is then achieved by spirituality and marriage by the Holy Spirit. A neglectful father cannot instruct positive decision-making; only a married or present father in a home can give the child the necessary discipline and nurture.

A leader wants a child of proven character, but first, he shows his child how to prove their character. Yahweh gave us the responsibility of being leaders, whether in prison or not. Fathers still have responsibilities and opportunities to lead our children by what we receive from our fathers; what we pass on to our children is our family heritage and legacy.

Inheritance of character, standards, values, and sense of identity installed in us, legacy is all of those characteristics inherited by our children installed by us from parents. We want to leave our children a solid spiritual and moral foundation that they can continue in a healthy family tree; this is our legacy in character, values, and leadership. We can pass along roots in spirituality, strong character, and strong values.

Greatness is defined by the number of people we serve. Serving others demonstrates true authority, and as fathers, we are called to help our children discover who they are and what they are dedicated to becoming. One of the most important things we can teach our children is the power of prayer. Alongside prayer, they should develop relationships, life skills, and academic abilities. As fathers, we must lead our children to follow Yahweh, helping them cultivate their talents and preparing them for the path Yahweh has planned for their future.

The things of this world are temporary, but our relationship with Yahweh is eternal. Our bond with Yahweh must come first, followed by the service we provide to others. Our children need to understand that their worth is not based on performance but on the love and guidance we provide.

A true legacy involves our children knowing they have security in Yahweh, that Yahweh has their hearts and faith. We must assure our children that we love them and are proud of them, and more importantly, that Yahweh loves them. This knowledge will encourage them, even when we are not present. Allow the Holy Spirit to lead you.

Ask for Yahweh's guidance, trust in Him completely, and maintain communication with Yahweh and your children through prayer. Keep your children lifted up in prayer, ask Yahweh to love and lead your family, and commit to being a spiritual father. Follow Yahweh's direction in leading your children. Always remember that a man, a father, and a husband are important in the kingdom of God. No one is perfect, but all is forgiven if there is true repentance.

In the past, we were shown how to avoid destruction; today, we are learning what and who to follow to prevent destruction. Our lifestyle determines our outcome, and our flesh and spirit must align. We must always pray for the best while being prepared for the worst. In the end, Yahweh has the final say, and He awaits our seeking Him. We do not wait for His seeking or calling.

Negativity must not dominate your thoughts. Holding on to rage and frustration only leads to festering bitterness, especially when it stems from things beyond our control. Bottled-up anger can cause danger. The wounds of childhood carried into adulthood often lead to disaster, and understanding the history of a boy helps explain the man he becomes. The unrighteous are not permitted to walk inside the kingdom of God; they remain outside the gate, while only the righteous may enter. Entrance is not determined by race, gender, color, or deeds.

Negativity prevents us from reaching our full potential and hinders us from achieving our goals and dreams. Hard work involves pain, effort, and the struggle to survive, but it is necessary. Life offers two types of decision-making: permanent and temporary. We must realize there is only One who can provide comfort in our discomfort and peace in our times of discouragement and brokenness. We must let go of the past and embrace the present, understanding that it is our choice to either hold on to negativity or choose positivity.

Some believe it is easy, while others think it is impossible to resist negativity. But the key is knowing what the positives are in order to resist. Who are you when you are alone? Who are you when you are around others?

The flesh was created to give birth to flesh, but the spirit was placed within the flesh to eventually return to spirit. Flesh is limited, but the spirit is limitless. After our time in the flesh, we are given the choice to follow our own paths.

We must differentiate between opinions, limits, and stress, and facts, determination, and success. Hurt needs love to heal. This is how a prince becomes a king, and a servant becomes a master—by turning darkness into light and death into life. Walk in the light where Yahweh can heal you. A prayerful boy becomes a spiritual man in the midst of spiritual warfare. Prayer guides our hearts and minds, transforming us from the death of the carnal mind to the life of the spiritual mind.

Our ancestors relied on strength, ability, and skill, but they also relied on Yahweh. Strength is drawn equally from both the natural and the supernatural. Love is shown through presence and affection, such as a simple hug. On the other hand, weakness is evident in homosexuality, which are lies created that populate our existence by genocide and extinction.

Men are to pass lessons down to boys. We must recognize problems within them before they become extra problems. Celebration is portrayed as bitterness in rejection, jealousy, love, and priority comes with maturity as the prince grows into the king or the princess grows into the queen. Changes and values will no longer be important; discussions will be arguments. The discussion deals with agreement and disagreement,. Arguments deal with blaming and creating more negativity.

Men and women handle fear and rejection differently— men tend to approach these issues logically, while women often respond emotionally. However, both sexes can be deeply affected and paralyzed by pain. Problems begin when people of each sex try to change the person they fell in love with versus trying to fully understand them as their partner. They choose when good doesn't match bad.

The greatest gift you can give a person is yourself -- although finances and fun can be added. That's how you elevate from couples to spouses because love and patience are everything. Trusting Yahweh turns negatives into positives, and mistakes become miracles. Men are to protect and provide. Women are to love and nurture. The goal is to change all negativity. Boys need to be accepted and taught how to treat others. That's how men become great, or they will only learn from experience.

A person's character shows how they were carried, helped, and who they believed in or trusted. Success means nothing without a successor. That's the greatest gift you can leave or compliment you can pass on. Fathers create other fathers who are apprentices. Men have fallen from their responsibility to show our youth how to become and be better than the previous generation. Men need to embrace their masculinity instead of femininity. Our men have been stolen by Satan's selfishness, sadness, and relations. We need to get them back to leading and showing equality, excitement, and passion in romance.

A fallen man is not beneath a strong man; hiding your true self won't show character. Being yourself brings the love of who you are. Hiding brings the love of what you can do. Yahweh knows your heart, mind, and intentions. He just loves for you to speak it.

Three stages of life are when teaching begins: childhood, teenage, and adulthood. During each stage, you learn differently. In childhood, you learn the basics and the beginning. In teenage you learn the importance and love. And in adulthood, you learn how to apply all you've learned and how to obtain and maintain life. A person's past should provoke them to teach the next generation to do better. We must teach that money is not to be worshipped but handled as a necessity.

Most great leaders have once been great followers. Children need to understand that marriage is a covenant—a bond and spiritual agreement worth fighting for. It is important to recognize that healing occurs at different rates for everyone, which requires patience. We must focus on acknowledging change, development, and comfort rather than resorting to criticism.

To embrace new beginnings, we must possess courage, commit fully to our spirit, and act as true warriors for Yahweh, not merely pretend ones. Even a faltering prayer can be as meaningful as a steady one, serving as a sincere compliment to Yahweh. Actions and experiences are the greatest teachers; words merely explain our actions or thoughts. Obedience is closely aligned with a hallelujah, the highest praise to Yahweh.

A wife needs her husband's security to find peace, while a child relies on their guidance and leadership to feel secure and reflect a positive image of Yahweh.

Prayer enables Yahweh to perform miracles and bestows prosperity upon those who have faith in His name. Strive to be the man you wish for your daughter to accept and marry and the example you want your son to follow. Giving is an opportunity to share the fruits of the spirit, which become blessings.

Fellowship guides us to the rock. Do not be overwhelmed; the spirit is working within you. Boys are meant to respect men, but respect is often lacking in today's world.

Tithing is a way of giving back to Yahweh and helping others. Giving is not limited to finances; it includes acts of worship such as singing, prayer, and dance. Only a blessed man can truly be in authority and under authority. A woman will only submit to a man who submits to Yahweh. To receive blessings, you must believe, maintain faith, and hope. It is impossible to succeed alone; grace and mercy lead to exceptional prayer and praise. A fallen man loses himself, while a risen man finds his true self. He can share his secrets, failures, and fears as part of a motivational lesson, remaining faithful and honest while providing a safe space grounded in values and morals. Yahweh heals any broken person who allows Him to; sometimes our direction and thoughts need healing so that prayer can serve as medicine for the spirit.

Embracing a multiracial and multicultural perspective fosters reconciliation and survival in our challenging times, allowing us to receive blessings in diverse ways. People worship in various forms—through bowing, shouting, or simply standing—and our responsibility is to guide others to the truth that we are one body in Christ. We should be able to share one plate and drink from one cup.

Unfortunately, mankind has become imprisoned by his own mind, heart, and emotions due to lost faith, differing preferences, agendas, and criticism. Segregation, alienation, separation, bondage, and a lack of love have hardened many hearts and blocked their blessings. A person of understanding is wise and receives the gifts of salvation, grace, and favor.

Before we can fulfill the work Yahweh has for us in heaven, we must diligently perform our tasks on earth. Yahweh knows our true identities, understanding us completely. Jobs we obtain should be maintained until we reach the career meant for us. Education is a fundamental necessity that complements all credentials, as morals, values, and standards influence how we dress and perform. Hard work reveals skill and character.

Comparing ourselves to others or our jobs often leads to falsehood; instead, maintaining composure and focus demonstrates dedication and responsibility, earning respect and trust. Gaining confidence in your field comes from learning, not pride.

Bills must be paid, and food must be provided; every man should have a vision so his partner can dream and support him in providing for their family. While working for the benefit of your family may spark jealousy in others, maintaining a positive attitude is crucial for securing great references. Effective communication is essential for navigating life, and comfort and awareness of your surroundings help demonstrate positivity. Ethics, defined by respect and gratitude earned from coworkers, managers, and bosses, plays a crucial role in progress.

The diverse characteristics of every ethnicity contribute to better futures for our youth, preparing them to become the next generation of leaders, role models, and beacons of hope through education, work, and entrepreneurship. Weakness in work ethic often stems from ineffective teaching and a lack of consistent, positive guidance. A person's limits are shaped by their decisions, actions, and beliefs. Falling does not mean one cannot rise again; hardships teach us to protect and provide for our families.

In the modern world, resources and opportunities are continually created, urging us not to waste blessings on foolishness. Mankind's greatest fear often stems from what they do not understand. We were created for greatness, with a purpose to fulfill and a mission to accomplish.

Throughout history, remarkable individuals have demonstrated this truth. Harriet Tubman fought courageously for freedom; Malcolm X and Martin Luther King Jr. championed equal rights and justice; Rosa Parks stood firm for respect and equality; George Washington Carver innovated with peanuts to create valuable products; and Madam C.J. Walker revolutionized hair care with her pioneering styling tools.

We were made to populate the earth and support one another, living temporarily in the flesh with the ultimate goal of transitioning into the Spirit. Our actions and achievements should reflect our divine purpose and commitment to serving one another and fulfilling our roles in God's plan. Racism and biases were taught to separate different neighborhoods for negative intentions instead of positive ones. Parents should have their children's best interest of well-being. We must love and support our family. A family should only be created when your financial plan is progressing. Action is needed in culture, human knowledge, belief, and behavior of man's learning.

Picking up our fellow man and not being judgmental conquers respect. Obedience in love, compassion, honor, and respect aren't taught on the streets. Showing certain behaviors can change a person's perception of life.

Public schools aren't taught like private. A parent's behavior is displayed through the actions of their children. Therefore, your children need to be taught proper conversation, counting money, following rules, and what those rules are or look like. The body must remain strong through the mind to be productive.

Corruption comes in the form of crime, broken families, violence, unrest, unrestrained, and negativity. Parents must improve their status, leave an inheritance, and obtain a better understanding of lifestyle so children view things differently. Life is more than drug deals, gangs, and handouts.

The only way to a better life is to teach what not to do, such as robbery, put-downs, stealing, and killings, which only bring suffering. Freedom to recreate is given up for violence. It takes more than one man or a few men to change our youth. Careers need to be chosen over drugs, family over gangs, father over absence, and responsibility over excuse. Action shows an effort to better the children of today to create a better tomorrow.

8

Three Stones of Foundation: A Man of Spirituality

Integrity

The heart of who Devin Sr. is as a man and father is trustworthy and honorable. Completeness, moral innocence, fullness, perfection, and simplicity in doing the right thing even when no one seems to be watching.

"The righteous man walks in integrity; his children are blessed after him."

(Proverbs 20:7)

"Whoever walks in integrity walks securely, but he who walks crooked will be found out."

(Proverbs 10:9)

Joseph was a man of integrity. *Read (Genesis 39).*

We often worry about our past failures, but there is greater hope. (1 John) The blood of Yahweh cleanses us from all sin. (2 Corinthians) If anyone is in Yahweh, he is a new creation; old things have passed away, and all things have become new.

It's both a great responsibility and an opportunity to teach, love, nurture, and grow. It's the first line in ministry: our role as fathers never ends. It's the most valuable asset in society.

Receive Yahweh's love, instructions, discipline, and example as a son of His, then it can be passed on to our children. Self-control is one of the aspects of the fruits of the Spirit. It's important to grow in maturity as men and dads. As we raise our children, we want to be faithful in our walk and words to be a good example and to provide wise advice.

For as many are led by the Holy Spirit, these are the sons of Yahweh. You did not receive the spirit of bondage to fear, but you received the spirit of adoption by whom we cry out, "Abba, Father." (Romans 8:14-15)

Yahshua was the first man of integrity. *Read (2 Corinthians 5:21)*

"I am the vine, you are the branches, he who abides in me, and I in him bears much fruit; for without me, you can do nothing. Life flows from the vine to the branch and brings grapes. Life flows from Yahweh to us and brings spiritual fruit."

(John 15:5)

"In him dwells all fullness of the Trinity bodily; and you are complete in him, who is the head of all principality and power."

(Colossians 2:9-10)

We are fully supplied by Yahshua! Although we fail, we can ask Yahweh to remove past failures by forgiveness. He will empower us to walk with integrity. Talk about being honest; also practice honesty with children. *1ˢᵗ Stone of Foundation.*

<u>Love</u>

The most important thing we can give our children, partners, and spouses is love because love is the greatest of Yahweh's qualities. When children know you love them, they feel accepted, partners stick by being helpful, and spouses will be committed to visions and dreams. Agape is the greatest love to give and receive; love is displayed in five other ways.

Giving is the way to real joy, peace, and happiness. Patience requires us to die for our own self-interest. Kindness involves compliments and gifts of affirmation. Discipline protects out of love; it doesn't anger anyone.

Forgiving underserved grace, nothing earned, removing bitterness and anger. *2nd Stone of Foundation.*

<u>Leadership</u>

Our calling is not just to tell what needs to be done but to be an example and show what needs to be done. The main skills children need to become our future leaders are relationships, life, and academics. Yahweh helps us to aid them in obtaining and maintaining those abilities. As we pray and lean on the Holy Spirit, we should enjoy our responsibilities as a servant leader in our homes.

Yahweh helps us to love and lead our families one by one and teach our children and others. They need to feel loved and important, knowing that we are proud of them. *3rd Stone of Foundation.*

Examples of leadership can be found in (John 13:13-17, Luke 22:24-26, Proverbs 22:6, John 17:3, and Proverbs 3:5-6).

9

Recovery

Accountability

Only Yahweh can offer us the power we need for recovery through Yahshua, the Messiah. If we look to any other source for help, our recovery will be limited. Christ-centered recovery is often doubted by many who need it the most. When people find deliverance through Christ, they are often told it's all a lie. Truth is deliverance leading to our recovery and restoration through Yahweh, the Messiah.

Many children who grow into adults are led to believe they are worthless to other people and insignificant to Yahweh. The Messiah came to save the lost, no matter how insignificant they are or become. Yahweh doesn't want anyone to miss the opportunity for salvation or recovery. Each one of us is valued no matter how painful our past or how far we have strayed. If we admit our needs and seek to follow His will for us, we will discover how important we are to Yahweh and those close to us. Yahweh wants us to have the proper attitude towards money and possessions and to utilize them unselfishly to help others in need. Knowing when to forgive and to confront is critical to the recovery process.

Yahshua taught that we are to freely and frequently extend forgiveness to others, sometimes even with tough love. If others are acting contrary to the Word, they need to be confronted for their own good. Strong drinks or drugs should never be offered in the recovery process. Those who offer these seek punishment from Yahweh. In recovery, not everyone appreciates efforts to intervene on their behalf. Those who are grateful are faithful and get well as they seek scripture.

Be cautious not to reject messages simply because they are uncomfortable or unwelcome. The path to victory often involves challenges and hardships, including those that we might prefer to avoid. Quick and easy solutions to recovery rarely yield lasting results. Instead, it is crucial to follow Yahweh's direction through His Word and counsel, even when the journey is long and demanding. Trusting in false alliances or relying on unreliable human sources of strength can lead to further suffering rather than true recovery.

Yahweh holds us accountable for our actions. Many of us have suffered innocently at the hands of others. Blaming others for their or our mistakes isn't validation. We can't change others' behaviors or how they treat us, but we can forgive them and put the pain of the experience behind us. In recovery, we must accept responsibility for the reaction behind the action and make amends to those harmed. Yahweh takes no pleasure in the death of the wicked. We were created to be responsible individuals, not to suffer. Yahweh desires that we choose Him. The result of not turning from sin is eternal separation. If we confess our sins, He will help us rebuild our lives no matter how extensive the devastation.

Spiritual rebirth is a necessity to the recovery process as it is to enter the kingdom. Being born again is the beginning. It's hard each day as we submit our stubborn hearts and wills to the control of the Holy Spirit. True recovery is not obtained through trying harder but by repentance and entrusting our lives to Yahweh in obedience to receive forgiveness. We are helpless sinners unable to affect our own recovery. Faith delivers us from the ultimate consequences of sin, and it also empowers us to make changes in our present. We are given a new identity when we turn to Yahweh's will to be children of light. Those who can admit the truth about themselves will have their eyes opened.

When certain circumstances no longer tempt us, we will need to be sensitive to others so they aren't led away and avoid activities that will lead to downfall. The more mature we are, our response to people will be loving. Many think it's easier to point out the failures of others instead of fixing their own failure. We visit Yahweh individually.

As we progress in recovery, we are to reach out to others; our deliverance can help them turn their lives around. Our progress can help others seek recovery. If we hide from our mistakes, they can haunt us, causing painful consequences of unchecked dependencies. As we turn our lives over to Yahweh, He starts our solid foundation. Many wonder how entrusting our lives to Yahweh can change anything. They find it embarrassing at times. True understanding can only be found by taking steps to obey Yahweh as we put aside analyzing and trying to understand so that we can experience Yahweh's healing power through simple faith and obedience. We will all stand before the gates of heaven to be judged by our good and bad actions while on earth. Although we fall short at times, we are no longer defined by our addictions; we are all forgiven, cleansed, and holy.

Loyalty

By confessing our sins and repenting, we receive Yahweh's forgiveness and cleansing. Our sins are forgotten and removed "as far from us as the east to the west." We have no reason to be reminded of our past when Yahweh has forgiven and forgotten our sins. When the past is brought up, there is no need to feel guilty; guilt leads to living in the past.

A true friend will stick beside you during hard times. Without relationships, recovery and growth can't take place. We all need to be able to express our needs and concerns to someone who will care, pray, and encourage us in our efforts to change.

Each day, we deal with things we cannot change. There will always be circumstances and situations beyond our control. We must also face the reality of who we are: human beings confined to each day. Escaping reality is part of the insanity program (addictive behavior).

"Do not worry about tomorrow; tomorrow will worry about itself; today has its own troubles…" [223] Yahweh's grace comes in daily doses;

---

[223] Matthew 6:34

face life day by day. Each day is a new opportunity to find joy, strength, and sanity as we accept realities.

Are you accepting the present moment or trying to escape into the past or future? Can you add anything to life?

A wonderful reward awaits those who have endured in faith. Full recovery is available only through that faith. Many with a dysfunctional background struggle to determine which behaviors and attitudes are acceptable; Yahweh can guide us. We can be confident that Yahweh's presence and power are available to help us practice the right living. Many of us in recovery may have difficulty dealing with authority figures. But we must remember the importance of leadership in others' lives, especially those who model godliness and are concerned about spiritual growth.

If our human leaders fail or are abusive, Yahshua is consistent and trustworthy. He will always be there for us as a God and friend. He deserves to receive all covenants equally. Praise for who he is, what he does, good works and services, and sharing with others in need; telling what he has done in our lives helps us to reach out to people in dire need.

Unlike human fathers, Yahweh helps His children to succeed by equipping them with the will of the Holy Spirit. Yahweh will provide us with all we need to overcome our dependencies by grace and mercy.

<u>Respect</u>

We are helpless and need to give our situations over to Yahweh, recognizing that we are giving Him control. We need to let Yahweh do things His way and in His time. Our past mistakes blind us to our present gifts. We must see ourselves as Yahweh sees us. The process we face in recovery may also be difficult, but no matter the pain, it is worth reaching the point of freedom and blessings.

Fidelity in marriage is central to Yahweh's plan for a family. Marriage is a bond of foundational building blocks. Adultery is a violation of trust and is part of the Ten Commandments.

Healthy relationships require self-control and respect for boundaries. Yahweh's intentions were not to deprive us. For marriage to bring joy and fulfillment, we were commanded to be holy and to respect our spouse and parents in holiness. A dysfunctional family can become one of the worst barriers to life, but we must seek fulfillment and contentment.

Yahweh desires that priority of respect be within families as the Israelites were commanded to give special consideration to the poor and underprivileged among them. Today, physical, emotional, and spiritual acceptance can be met in the atmosphere of love. Yahweh demands honesty in both word and deed. Dishonesty and misrepresentation lead to suspicion, mistrust, and hatred, ultimately destroying our relationships. Human relationships can grow and thrive only if we are willing to tell the truth. When there is honesty in our relationships, we can confidently seek others. The advice given needs to be assessed, even from close friends; we must be tuned in to what Yahweh desires for a particular situation, not what might be the easy way out.

When life gets out of control, family tension and conflict are common. Home should be a place where love and mutual respect are shown. Husbands and wives should love one another and be sensitive to needs; this shows the love of the Messiah within the church. Pain is created when addictions take over by selfishly seeking to meet self-needs. Neglect and hurt are gained by the people who seek love and support.

Rebuilding a family relationship is the most important task we face in recovery; admitting wrongs and seeking to make amends to loved ones can reestablish mutual love and respect. Parents and children are to show love to each other. Also, children are to honor their parents.

Today, children often show disrespect toward their parents, leading to a rift through ridicule and neglect that can leave lasting scars. Both parents and children have fallen short, and reconciliation requires acknowledging these failures. We must recognize the unseen spiritual warfare waged by Satan against us. Many struggles with addiction may stem from direct attacks by spiritual entities, exacerbating our dependencies and rendering us powerless.

By admitting our struggles and surrendering our lives to Yahweh, we find assurance that He will stand with us in this battle. Yahweh's armor provides protection in the physical realm. In accepting the sword of the Word, recovering addicts need to cultivate awareness of Yahweh, surrounding themselves with truth, righteousness, faith, and prayer. These elements defend against spiritual assaults.

While the forces we face are powerful, Yahweh's armor offers us the strength needed for adequate defense. The shoes of peace enable us to spread the good news of Yahweh, providing hope to others as we continue our journey of recovery.

Our personal inventory needs to be taken; it requires self-discipline, spiritual strength, and agility, and can only come through practice. We need to develop our spiritual muscles through consistent daily scripture. Like athletes have weights and workout routines, we can benefit in this life and one to come with patience because results don't necessarily show up overnight. Continual practice and discipline each day will eventually reap full benefits.

We need to make direct amends except when it will injure others. Attitudes, addictions, and selfishness were once shown until consideration was given. This shows others that their interests and needs matter. Don't try to impress others. Be humble. Whether we make amends directly or choose not to make amends because of injury, it can save a lot of pain and suffering. Situations may occur when we make amends. If suffering occurs, doing good and being patient is enduring, and Yahweh is pleased. The Messiah also suffered; Yahshua did not retaliate when insulted nor threaten revenge for suffering.

Yahshua left the judgment to Yahweh, who judges fairly. The difficulty comes from the consequences of past actions.

Trust

Yahweh assures He cares by listening to us alone, as Satan tries to plant thoughts of hopelessness in our minds and tell us that we have gone too far for Yahweh to forgive us. Yahshua is our advocate and has already paid the price of our failures. The evidence of salvation in a person's life is love for others shown in action, not just words.

An important part of recovery is being willing to extend Yahweh's love to others as Yahweh has shown His love. In the middle of insanity, He loved us, using enough to free us from bondage and using us to show His love towards others in need of recovery.

False teachers have claimed that moral restraint is unnecessary, arguing that what one does in the flesh is inconsequential. Those who followed this teaching became indifferent to sin, reverting to old, sinful habits and believing it was acceptable. Anything that leads us away from Yahweh is out of bounds.

Staying focused on Yahweh is essential for spiritual growth and maturity. True faith encompasses intellectual, social, and emotional satisfaction within spiritual recovery. It occurs when these aspects of life are centered on genuine faith in Yahweh. Addressing our shortcomings and making amends is possible when we confront all areas of our lives.

There is a stark contrast between the light of Yahweh and the darkness of Satan. Honest self-examination and accurate personal inventory are crucial for spiritual growth. Choosing to live in the light and continually acknowledging our flaws will result in a cleansed conscience and a fulfilling relationship with Yahweh. Our assurance is confirmed by our persistence and willingness to follow Yahweh's will. Those who claim salvation but persistently disobey Yahweh are deceiving themselves. Recovery is impossible without submitting to

Yahweh's guidance. This involves maintaining personal inventory, admitting our wrongs to others, and confessing our sins to Yahweh.

As our love for Yahweh deepens, our actions will reflect this love. A key sign of true faith is the love we show to others. Hatred or animosity indicates that recovery has not yet begun. Light and darkness cannot coexist in the same heart; the absence of love will hinder our progress in recovery. Demonstrating love for others is not a weakness but a sign of emotional strength. The love of Yahweh empowers us to make amends with those we have wronged and those who have wronged us.

Yahshua is our high priest who advocates for us, making His will known to us and our heartfelt needs known to Yahweh. Yahshua's words and deeds reveal Yahweh's mercy, justice, glory, and truth. His words reveal His desire to establish a personal relationship with each of us as He intercedes on our behalf, bringing our needs and requests continually before Yahweh. He prays that we would know His perfect joy, be protected from all evil, grow in truth and holiness, and show love towards all people.

Real love brings security into our lives. Feelings of insecurity contribute to the power of our dependencies. Believing that love can bring lasting security may be hard for those who have been abandoned. Someone may betray our trust; we may have betrayed theirs. Someone we needed may have died, leaving us permanently.

The love of Yahweh remains forever with those who fear Him. Yahweh's love helps to avoid relapse. It meets us at our deepest need and overcomes our most powerful insecurities. As the light of the world, Yahshua exposes what has been hidden and guides us down the path of life and recovery.

In part, to walk in the light means to be honest and vulnerable with others and to walk in fellowship with Yahweh. As we express our needs and feelings and our sins and struggles with the people we trust, light will fall on our failures and strengths, giving us the direction we need to make significant progress in recovery. To be set free is to know the truth about ourselves and about Yahshua, our liberator. We are in bondage to sin and powerless to manage our lives effectively. We can recognize and confess our needs and struggles, our sins and addictions, with our moral inventory. When we turn our broken lives over to Yahweh, who alone can make us whole, we are acknowledging the truth – combining truth to set us free from sinful habits.

Changing patterns of behavior that led us into bondage or recovering from emotional trauma requires the help of people we trust and respect. We cannot successfully live alone. Wise people listen to good advice from others; fools do not. Growing towards spiritual and emotional maturity is a process that requires the help of trustworthy people who can guide us with care and hold us accountable as we try to make changes.

It is foolish to lose our temper when we are insulted. We demonstrate maturity by using self-control and staying calm. By doing so, we can offer needed correction to the offender– providing a chance to build intimacy in the relationship and keep our hearts free of resentment.

People who deceive, slander, lie, and encourage others to follow immoral lifestyles cannot ignore Yahweh's Word for long. Yahweh sees what goes on. And just because He is silent doesn't mean He doesn't care. One day, He will present His case against them, and their judgment will be final. If we fail to admit and confess our sins, they will continue to burden us with destructive guilt and rob us of joy. We need to learn to confess and forsake our sins immediately. Then, we need to seek Yahweh's wisdom as to how we can make amends for the wrongs we have done to others. We won't be able to progress in the recovery process or reach out to others until we seek forgiveness for our past failures.

Some people may not readily forgive, but we can be sure Yahweh will. If we try to hide or deny our sins, we are in grave danger of judgment. If we are sensitive to our sins and humbly seek Yahweh's forgiveness, there is hope for us. No matter how great our past sins are, Yahweh will remove any guilt and restore joy.

<u>Unity</u>

Reconciling our human relationships is an important part of the recovery process. We need the people in our lives to give us encouragement to overcome our pain and to stand with us against the temptations we face. There is nothing like human fellowship and friendship, and Yahweh wants to bless us through other people. The kind of friends most helpful to us in recovery are those who are trying to live spiritual lives. Knowing that Yahweh has chosen us as His own should give us the confidence to call on Him when we are in trouble. All through the earth, He can help us when we call on Him in his greatness. No problem is too great for Him.

Yahshua makes His will known to us and our heartfelt needs known to Yahweh. Yahshua's words and deeds reveal Yahweh's assessment of our strengths and weaknesses, teaching us humility as we uncover our sins and faults. It will also help us develop a grateful attitude toward Yahweh as we discover the many gifts He has given us. Yahweh has an important role for each of us, even though we may wonder how He could use us. We may feel isolated, useless, and alone, but we were all given special gifts that are needed by others.

Part of recovery involves sharing our stories of deliverance with others. It could mean the difference between life and death for someone in need. As we reach out to encourage others, our isolation will give way to fellowship. Yahweh tells us to let love govern all our attitudes and actions; this certainly applies to the process of recovery. We are called to evenly love our enemies. We have all been wronged by others, and Yahweh's love allows us to forgive them and reconcile.

Love enables us to ask for their forgiveness and seek to make amends for the trouble and pain we have caused. Often, we need to make a special effort to reach out to immediate family: parents, siblings, children, or spouses. Love in action is not easy; it demands that we set our pride aside and admit our wrongs to each other. As painful as love can be, it is the only way to experience the joy of rebuilding our relationships and progress in recovery.

The government was set in place by Yahweh. Therefore, we must submit to the government as we were submitting to Yahweh. Often, we suffer from great abuse by authority. We think -- why submit to authorities who do not act wisely or justly?

Sometimes, we need to resist the injustices that are being done against us. We can do this by communicating with trustworthy people about abusive situations. We are called to support and obey authorities that seek to uphold justice. When they stand in direct contradiction to their oath, we need the support of others to try to change the situation.

Progress in recovery can take place only as we learn to love others. People must realize love is not an emotion we feel; it is an attitude and outpouring of unselfish concern for others. If we love Yahweh and the people around us, we will treat them with respect. We would never steal from them. We would not harm them in any form, shape, or fashion to satisfy our own selfish desires.

As we continue to take personal inventory, we can use love as the standard by which we judge our behavior. If we measure all our actions against Yahweh's standard of love, we will experience great progress in recovery and our relationships. We can't give people, religious leaders, or leaders in recovery the position of Yahweh by believing everything they say or perhaps do.

People are powerless and often make temporary use of Yahweh's direction. We must measure everything we hear against the truth of Yahweh's word. We only need a willing heart to receive Yahweh's power and forgiveness. People have no power or ability that can ultimately overcome the powers of sin in our lives. A life of self-sufficiency is ultimately self-destructive. When we turn our lives over to Yahweh, we accept His way. Only then can we experience Yahweh's power.

We have been gifted in ways that make us necessary to others. Others have been gifted in ways that make them necessary to us. Some have gifts of teaching about Yahweh. Gifts are important for spiritual growth. Yahweh has a purpose for all individuals and desires us to be in a community to strive to know Him better through prayer and meditation on His word. He will show us what our gifts are and how we can use them to help others; as we share our gifts, we can help others. Sharing gifts and benefits will help us grow stronger and full of love.

A life of recovery is the commitment to knowing Yahweh better. In examining our lives, we realize just how demanding Yahweh's standards for righteous living are. Yahweh's grace helps us conform to His will. As we obey Him, we are taught to live without bitterness, anger, or harsh words. He is in the business of healing us. Following Yahweh's way, we are on our way to reconciliation -- building a solid foundation for recovery. We are to avoid sexual immorality, greed, and harsh language since they are not part of Yahweh's character.

Our spiritual awakening will lead us to feel a growing concern for people in need. As we share the message of hope with others, we should also pray for their progress as part of serving them. Our prayer for other people struggling with addiction will impact their spiritual growth. Our personal stories of deliverance are an essential tool for reaching others in need of recovery. A painful past and powerful deliverance open the door to our serving. We cannot lose if we belong to Yahweh.

Whether we live or die, we know we will win in the end. During times of relapse and failure, we are tempted to give up on life completely. But no matter how bad things are, if we trust Yahweh, He will come through for us. We will have one more victory story to share with others. Yahweh uses us to save the lives of others equal to our own given reason to live.

As members of the body of Christ, we are deeply connected to one another. When others in our community are hurt, we feel their pain as well. Early in the recovery process, it may be necessary to focus on our own well-being. However, as we progress, we should move beyond self-centeredness and become more concerned with the well-being of others. Part of making amends to those we have harmed involves demonstrating that we have changed. As our relationships strengthen, our addictions will gradually lose their hold on us.

Yahshua is the ultimate model of humility, obedience, and service. His example of humbly obeying Yahweh is a powerful lesson for us. As we take an honest, moral inventory of our lives, we must admit our faults with humility, which allows us to begin changing our destructive patterns. Embracing humility and admitting our failures without hesitation will support our recovery journey. Obedience is essential for spiritual growth, and we are given the desire and ability to obey through reading the Word and spending time in prayer. Transformation from the inside out helps us shine brightly through maintaining faith. This requires stamina and a servant's attitude to succeed in our spiritual battles.

We must dedicate ourselves to the cause of Christ, placing others' needs above our own comforts as we share the message of salvation and recovery with those who struggle. By surrendering our desires to meet the needs of others, we also release the burden of our addictions. Serving others helps us build meaningful relationships and establishes a solid foundation for lasting recovery. In helping others, we ultimately help ourselves.

Arguments

As we get further along in recovery, the memories of how bad our lives really were may begin to fade. When we take the message of recovery to others, we must never forget where we came from and how we got where we are. Once, we were foolish and disobedient; we were misled and became slaves to many lusts and pleasures. When Yahshua revealed his kindness and love, he saved us -- not because of the righteous things we had done, but because of his mercy. He washed away our sins, giving us a new birth and new life through the Holy Spirit.

As we share our message, let us never forget the following truths: Our lusts and pleasures once ruled over us just as they rule over others today. Our hearts were filled with confusion and painful emotions that others still feel. We were saved because of the love and kindness of Yahweh, not because we were good enough. We must also remember that we can stay free with Yahweh upholding us and staying with us.

Pride can lead individuals to hide behind defenses during the recovery process. People may conceal their true selves behind good reputations, prestigious positions, or a facade of superiority. Some might feel such deep inner shame that they go to great lengths to project a self-righteous public image. Those who have attempted to protect themselves in these ways need a profound change in attitude.

Yahshua exemplifies the attitude we should adopt: He relinquished His divine privileges, took on the humble position of a servant, and was born as a human. In His human form, He humbled Himself in obedience to Yahweh, enduring the cross. As a result, He was exalted to the highest honor and given the most exalted name. He endured the cross to sit in the place of honor beside Yahweh's throne.

Yahweh has the power to transform attitudes and remove pride, preventing people from hiding behind masks. Embracing everyone's struggles with addiction and yielding to Yahweh in recovery leads to future honor and the restoration of a good name. True illumination comes when lives are surrendered to Yahweh, revealing self-truth and shedding evil deeds for a life of decency. No one is without sin, but forgiveness is granted through confession and repentance.

A crucial step in recovery is recognizing that many of our sins were committed unconsciously, requiring deep soul-searching to uncover. We can be assured that each time we confess our sins, Yahweh will forgive them. Seeking revenge will never resolve anger; it only perpetuates more ill will. The true resolution comes when both parties move beyond the origin of the conflict.

Anger can be overcome by forgiving those who have hurt us and addressing the conflict with love and mutual respect. Sin can be relinquished by entrusting matters to Yahweh for ultimate justice. Sin causes pain in others' consciences, revealing what is wrong. Therefore, confess, repent, and be forgiven.

In recovery, there is no need to dwell on past mistakes. Recovery requires care, prayer, and encouragement. Nourishing the mind with knowledge of Yahweh's plan is essential. We must love to study His Word, drawing ourselves away from the unhealthy and toward what is true, honorable, right, pure, lovely, and admirable. Growth involves being accountable and receptive to constructive criticism. One should seek feedback from respectful individuals to learn from mistakes and develop understanding and maturity.

Yahweh knows the true motives behind our actions and excuses, and He is the only one who can make recovery possible. A friend is someone outside of family, spouse, or lover whose company you enjoy and for whom you feel genuine affection. A true friend will always want you to succeed and will support you in achieving that success. An associate, on the other hand, is a person connected with others in a particular activity, enterprise, or business as a partner or colleague. Associates might be present for work, entertainment, or classroom settings but are generally concerned with their own benefits rather than their well-being.

10
Blessings

If you woke up this morning with more health than illness, there are others who won't last this week.

If you haven't experienced the danger of battle, the loneliness of imprisonment, the agony of torture, or the pangs of starvation, you are ahead of millions of people around the world.

If you attend church meetings without fear, arrest, torture, or death, you are ahead of billions of people in the world. If you have food in your refrigerator, clothes on your back, a roof over your head, and a place to sleep, you're richer than 75% of the world. If you have money in the bank, your wallet, and spare change, you are as wealthy as 8% of the world.

If your parents are married and alive, you are very rare. If you hold your head with a smile on your face, thankfully, you are blessed because most cannot. If you can hold someone's hand, hug them, or touch their shoulder, you are blessed because you can heal others.

If you have read this whole encouragement, you are more blessed than billions who can't read anything at all. You are blessed in the smallest ways to appreciate the biggest.

Transforming our minds involves self-control, desire, focus, and discipline. It is our human nature to seek pleasure instead of discomfort. To be a servant of Yahweh, we will undergo difficult tasks in life, and we should refrain from worldly temptations and fleshly desires.

Transforming the mind and developing self-control while in prison is an exceptionally challenging task. The prison environment tests every aspect of humility, making you question the goodness of life outside its walls. It often leaves you feeling abandoned, alone, and isolated. The system is designed to erode confidence and independence. It is profoundly difficult to live under constant control, where every aspect of your life is regulated—when you can speak on the phone, visit with family, seek knowledge, or pursue personal rehabilitation.

The opposite way of thinking is to rely on recognizing what is good and bad and learning how to be a man walking as one of Yahweh's children.

11

Yahweh Knows

When you are weary and disheartened by fruitless efforts, when your tears have flowed so long that your heart aches with anguish, and life feels suspended as time slips by, you may find yourself feeling lonely because others are too busy to notice. When you have tried everything and seem to have nowhere to turn, when nothing makes sense and confusion and frustration overwhelm you, remember this: your efforts have not gone unnoticed, your tears are counted, and you are not alone. He is waiting with you, standing by your side. He has a solution and holds the answer to your struggles.

You have a brighter outlook and pieces of hope; things are going well, and you have much to be thankful for. Something joyful happens, and you are filled with awe. You have a purpose to fulfill and a dream to follow. Yahweh has whispered to you, blessed you, smiled upon you, opened your eyes, and called you by name.

12

Answered Prayers

When the idea is not the best, when it's absolutely wrong, when it can help you but harm someone else, Yahweh says No.

If Yahweh answered every prayer at the snap of your finger, He would become your servant and not your master. Yahweh says Slow.

Yahweh's delays are not denials; it's timing. Patience is what's needed, along with prayer.

The selfish has to grow unselfish. The cautious has to grow courage. The timid has to grow confidence. The critical has to grow tolerance. The negative has to grow positive. And the seeker has to grow compassion for suffering. Yahweh says, Grow.

Miracles start to happen. An alcoholic is freed. A drug addict is released. Doubters gain belief. Diseases are healed. And closed doors become open doors. When everything is all right, Yahweh stands at the open door, saying, "Go."

13
ABCs of Yahweh

- **A**void negative sources (people, places, and habits)

- **B**elieve in Yahshua as your Messiah and Savior

- **C**onsider things from every angle

- **D**on't give up, and don't give in

- **E**njoy life today

- **F**amily and friends are hidden treasures

- **G**ive more

- **H**ang on to your dreams

- **I**gnore those who try to discourage you

- **J**ust do it if it pleases Yahweh

- **K**eep trying

- **L**ove Yahweh first

- **M**ake it happen

- **N**ever lie, cheat, or steal

- **O**pen your eyes and see things as Yahweh does

- **P**ray through everything

- **Q**uitters never win

- **R**ead your Bible

- **S**top procrastinating

- **T**ake Yahshua as your guide

- **U**nderstand yourself to understand others

- **V**isualize it

- **W**ant the Holy Spirit to change you

- **X** your efforts

- **Y**ou are unique

- **Z**ero in on your target and go for it

14
My Son

If you

Can keep your head when everyone around you is losing theirs and blaming it on you,

Can trust self when all doubt you,

Wait and not be tired of waiting,

Be lied to but not deal in lies,

Be hated but don't return hate, Not look too good nor talk too wise.

If you

Can dream and not make them your master,

Think and not make thoughts your aim,

Meet triumph and disaster, treating them the same,

Hear the truth, but be twisted to make a trap,

Watch the things you've given life to break, but build them back up with worn-out tools.

If you

Can make all your winnings and sacrifice it all,

Lose everything and start again at the beginning,

Never breathe a word about your loss,

Have heart and nerve long after they are gone,

Hold on when there is nothing in you,

If you

Can talk with crowds and keep your virtue; neither friends nor foes

can hurt you,

because All counts with you, but not very much.

Fill an unforgiven minute with seconds of forgiveness,

Then

Everything on the Earth is yours, and everything that is

in it,

as it was given to Man since the beginning of time,

My Son![224]

---

[224] From "If" by Rudyard Kipling, Copyright Credit: n/a

Conclusion

Our deepest fear is not that we are inadequate. Our deepest fear is that we are powerful beyond measure. It is our light, not our darkness, that frightens us the most. Playing small does not serve the world. There is nothing enlightened about shrinking so that other people will not feel insecure around you.

We are all meant to shine as children do. It is not just in some of us; it is in everyone. And as we let our own lights shine, we unconsciously give other people permission to do the same. As we are liberated from our own fear, our presence automatically liberates others.

–Marianne Williamson

<u>Certificate of Commitment:</u>

- My commitment to Yahweh. "For you are my rock and my fortress; and for your name's sake you lead me and guide me." *(Psalm 31:3)*

<u>My Commitment to My Children:</u>

Whereupon I believe that children are a blessing, I, Devin Nelson Sr., promise to commit the following scriptures to my heart and to obey them as I bring up my children with the help of Yahweh and my family:

- I will love my child unconditionally. *(Proverbs 3:12)*

- I will instruct my child according to the Word of Yahweh. *(Proverbs 22:6 and Isaiah 54:13)*

  I will discipline my child according to the scripture. *(Proverbs 29:17 and Ephesians 6:4)*

- I will honor my child. *(Psalms 127:3-5)*

- I will trust Yahweh for guidance. *(Proverbs 3:5 and Malachi 4:6)*

I pledge to you, my children, Alissa, Anastasia, Devin Jr., Destiny, and Da'mir, that I will faithfully, and to the best of my ability, carry out all the above with Yahweh's help while trusting Him for the results of my actions.

"If you could only sense how important you are to the lives of those you meet, how important you can be to the people you may never even dream of. There is something of yourself that you leave at every meeting with another person."

–Mister Rogers

Final Thoughts

My Journey into the Gospel was inspired by my spiritual brothers: Courtney S., Christian E., Jacob W., and all the other spiritual believers who surrounded me and considered following me. The ones who encouraged me to share my story, for all the churches I visited and grew up in Jesus, especially the Tabernacle of Deliverance, Pastor David Billy.

I am proud to be led by the Holy Trinity and to be a living child of Yahweh. I am grateful He has carried me as the "Footprints in the Sand" illustrates.

About the Author

Devin Sr. began writing *My Journey into the Gospel* in 2020 after feeling he had no one to turn to while incarcerated. Only hearing from a few people, he began to feel abandoned. Before incarceration, he sought the right path in life. He made a mistake that cost him a great deal of time in prison.

Devin Sr.'s aim is to show readers they can overcome and still dream while being incarcerated.

You can do anything you put your mind to in life. We must never let anyone tell us what we can't accomplish or what won't work. We must surround ourselves with positive people and steer clear of negativity around us.

Devin Sr. enjoys helping others avoid mistakes that can slow down and hinder their lives. He is a mentor, father, loved one, and advice seeker. He is a knowledge-sharing inspiration.

9 781969 775147